To all the staff of the
Nicholson-McKenzie Memorial Hospital
with grateful thanks from
Mollie Hunter

Part One
"The Enchanted Land"

1

It was the snow that began it all. "The cuckoo snow" they called it, because it was one of those late falls that can happen in April, when the cuckoo bird begins sending out its soft, insistent cry. But the two policemen on watch behind the hedge were unaware of this romantic notion and of the part the cuckoo snow had played in the capture they hoped to make. The policemen had a thief in their sights.

The thief was a small, female figure. She had her back to them and she was kneeling beside one of the rows of low, box-like structures – too far away from the policemen to allow them to see what she was actually doing there. But those structures were pens for breeding pheasants. And, the gamekeeper of the pheasant-breeding estate had complained, the pens were being robbed. Eggs were being taken from them, the eggs he should have had from the hen pheasants there. And what were the police going to do about that?

"We'll catch her," said one of the watching policemen, "red-handed!"

He was a big man with sergeant's stripes on his sleeve; and since kneeling behind a hedge did not come easily to him, his mood was not a pleasant one. The constable kneeling beside him was equally large, but being young and agile, his position was not causing him any great discomfort. More mildly than the sergeant had spoken, he asked:

"Who d'you think she is?"

"We'll find out soon enough. But I've heard that there's travelling families in the district – tinkers. And it's my guess she's from one of them."

Silently the constable acknowledged that this was a fair guess. All tinkers were thieves, after all – or so he had heard, at least. And who but a tinker child would be where this one was?

She was standing up now, looking around her. She whistled, and the whistle produced a big black dog from behind a clump of gorse bushes. The sergeant noted the dog as being a lurcher, cross-bred from a greyhound and some other strain and therefore typically a tinker's dog. It ran fast towards the girl, and something about its shuffling gait and the heavy set of its shoulders made him guess at Labrador as the other strain. A good cross, he thought, a good combination of speed with weight and scenting powers – and had to catch himself up with regret for the approval in the thought.

The girl stooped to pick some objects out of the snow, holding the front of her skirt up like an apron to receive them. With another whistle to the dog she moved off across the snow-covered field, holding the objects in the bunched-up front of her skirt.

She was heading for the road that ran along one side of the field, a dirt road that was part of the network connecting the various areas of the estate. The policemen glanced at one another, then rose on unspoken agreement and headed for their car.

The snow on the road was rutted by the tyres of the police car on its way to the gamekeeper's cottage. Catriona McPhie – "Cat" to her friends – walked along

4

one of the ruts, glad of the easy going made by the compressed snow underfoot; and as she walked she busied her mind by thinking ahead to her arrival at the travellers' camp.

Not that she hadn't enjoyed the morning so far, she told herself. Far from it! It had been great to wake up to the sight of the cuckoo snow, great to join all the other kids racing barefoot through it, squeezing the soft stuff up between her bare toes, yelling at the cold tingle against her warm skin. But the snow around the tents and trailers had soon become all churned up. And so it had been even better fun then to take off across the still-untouched whiteness beyond the camp, alone except for Shuffler running beside her – just the two of them in the whole, big, shining-white world of the cuckoo snow! And of course, if it hadn't been for the snow and her idea of enjoying it all by herself, she would never have discovered those pheasant pens.

But now she was cold. She had spent too long kneeling beside the pens watching the hen birds run back and forth, timidly, like pale brown shadows moving over the snow, too long admiring the strutting and the brilliant plumage of the cock birds. Her feet, especially, were cold. But that was her own fault, of course, for not having had the sense to put her shoes on before she ran off from the others. She was hungry too, now.

"So hungry," she informed Shuffler, "that my stomach thinks my throat's been cut."

Shuffler trotted on, unheeding. Cat took a peek into the folds of her bunched-up skirt, and smiled to think it was his scraping at a rabbit hole that had uncovered the bits of rock she had found there. A gleam of red winked up at her from among the folds of cloth – red of garnet embedded in those bits of greyish rock. And garnet, she had heard, was a gem-stone!

Happily, unaware that the garnet-bearing schist she carried was a common and worthless find, she gave herself up to dreams of the riches that would surely now be hers; and was so absorbed in these thoughts that she barely heard the snow-muffled sound from the tyres of the car that swept past her. The car drew to a halt immediately ahead of her and two men stepped out – two large men in the dark-blue uniforms of the police.

Polis! Cat stopped dead in her tracks, the traveller's automatic distrust of policemen making the word ring like an alarm bell in her mind. In swift, long strides the policemen were on her, the constable speaking as he came.

"Aye she's a tink, all right. See those bare feet – in the snow, too! And you said that tinkers were good to their bairns, whatever else they were!"

Shuffler backed away from the policemen, growling. Shuffler too, had learned to distrust men in blue uniforms. The sergeant loomed over Cat, one hand going up to smooth the ends of his long, fair moustache.

"All right, you. What's your name?"

Cat stood staring up at him, her mind suddenly filled with the dread of seeing him take out his little notebook and writing her name in it. That would be a terrible thing to happen, she reckoned – a black mark against her for the rest of her life, maybe! But how was she to avoid that?

"You heard me!" Pale blue eyes, bulbous, and bright with hostility glared down from above the hand stroking the moustache. Inspiration came suddenly to Cat.

"Er – Janet," she said. And then more boldly, "Janet Townsley." That would be all right, she reckoned. The

Townsleys were safely away in Argyllshire, hundreds of miles from this big sergeant of polis. And anyway, she had never heard of any Townsley called Janet.

"Townsley." The constable turned the name over on his tongue. "That's a tinker name, sure enough – eh, sergeant?"

The sergeant had been reaching for his notebook, but now his hand dropped from the pocket that held it. "Aye. But I doubt if it's hers. Look at that black hair she has. And the Townsleys are mostly fair-haired – white as lint, some of them are. Besides, it's usually in the south-west, around Argyllshire, that you get Townsleys. I tell you – " The sergeant was beginning to enjoy showing off his knowledge. Hands on hips now, rocking back on his heels, he glanced sideways at the constable. "I tell you, Miller, I know these traveller people. I know them. And this one's no more a Townsley than I am. But we'll get her real name out of her yet – down at the station maybe. And I'll bet you something, Miller. She's either a Stuart or a McPhie by the look of her, and so it's no wonder she's learned her tricks so early. How old would you say she is?"

The constable made a doubtful guess. "Ten?"

"I'm not!" Swiftly Cat contradicted him. "I'm eleven – nearly, anyway. At least – " With doubt overcoming her, she added hesitantly, "I think I am."

"You see!" The sergeant spoke triumphantly. "That's what they're like. That's what comes of their restless kind of life. They're not even sure of their own ages!"

The constable cleared his throat. "The – um – the eggs, sergeant?" Apologetically he gave the reminder, and sharply the sergeant told him:

"I was coming to that."

Cat felt a renewed prickle of alarm at the annoyance in the sergeant's voice. And what was the constable talking about – "eggs"? The sergeant was nodding towards her bunched-up skirt.

"All right, you – Stuart, McPhie, whatever your name is. Show me what you've got in there."

"Nothing." Cat tightened her clutch on her skirt. "At least – " She hesitated, afraid the sergeant would say she couldn't keep the garnets because she'd picked them up on private property. "It's just – just some wee bits of stone."

"You hear that, Miller?" The sergeant turned to the constable and gave a mock-sorrowful shake of the head. "Cunning as a barrowload of monkeys, these tinks are, even at this one's age. Though like as not she's been put up to this robbery by one of the older ones in their camp."

"But it's true," Cat protested. "Honest, it's just stones I have."

"D'you see the green in my eye?" The sergeant's lip curled satirically. "We were watching you at those pheasant pens, my girl. So come on, now. Show me those eggs you stole."

"I didn't! I didn't!" Cat's grip on her skirt became frantic. Her voice soared into a shout. "I haven't got any eggs!"

"We'll see about that!" The sergeant shot out a hand to grasp her shoulder. She ducked beneath his reach, twisted away from the constable's attempt to grab her, and took a flying leap down the embankment that carried the road across the field. She rolled head over heels, but with the snow cushioning the force of the fall, and was off again like a bullet out of a gun.

8

Shouts came winging after her, a succession of loud and angry shouts; but, she reckoned, those polis wouldn't try to follow her. Because they'd only be in trouble if they did, big heavy men like them, in big heavy boots. They'd sink right down in the snow, they would; right to their ankles in snow. And so she'd got safe away from them. *And* she still had her precious garnets!

The black form of Shuffler came circling towards her. Shuffler had already made his own quiet and cunning break. The shouts behind her were becoming more distant, were dying away altogether. Running fast and lightly, her steps just breaking the snow's crisp surface, Cat began casting on a wide track that would keep her well away from the estate road but would yet take her roundabout back to the camp. Shuffler veered to meet her on this track; and ten minutes later they had picked up the imprints left by their journey outwards from the camp that morning. Cat felt her hunger returning in full force then, but she was already running at full stretch and there was still half a mile to go to the woodland clearing that held the camp.

"I wish," she panted, "I wish, Shuffler, that I *had* pinched those damned eggs. I'd have them sucked dry by now!"

She topped a rise of ground, and in the hollow beyond saw three figures running towards her. They were strung out across the snow, two of them boys, the third a girl, with the girl trailing behind the other two. She waved, recognising them as her cousins, Rhona McPhie and Alec MacDonald, and the other boy as the more distantly-related Charlie Drummond. Alec, the oldest of the three, was the first to reach her.

"Where you been?" he panted. "Cat, where you *been?*"

9

"Talkin' to the polis." Charlie came up in time to hear her reply. She laughed at the frown it brought to his face, and teasingly continued, "They saw me at some pheasant pens and said I'd pinched the eggs. But trust me! I'm not daft. I got away from them all right."

"You *were* daft – to go near the pens in the first place." Charlie spoke with all the superiority conferred by his thirteen-year-old knowledge of such matters; but she had no time to think of any defence to this censure, because Rhona had now come panting up to join the group.

"Oh, Cat!" Rhona's face was twisted with some sort of distress that came from more than breathlessness. "Oh, Cat, why'd you run off the way you did?"

"I wanted to. There was all that snow around." Cat gestured to the snow-covered fields smoothly sweeping away on every side of them, and felt a swift, returning stab of the exhilaration that had been hers when she and Shuffler had run off together. "And mine," she added proudly, "was the very first foot to make a mark on it."

The other three exchanged glances. Then, in an oddly stiff way, Rhona said.:

"Your mammy sent me to look for you."

With a nod towards Rhona, Alec said, "And I came with her."

Charlie added, "And I chummed Alec."

Once again those glances, then silence, with all of them looking at the ground instead of at her.

"Well?" Cat stared at the group, wondering at the way they had spoken. That was always their habit, wasn't it – for Alec to follow where Rhona went, for Charlie to follow Alec? And so why were they bothering to tell her that now?

Somewhere inside her she felt a cold shiver of apprehension. Momentarily her sight seemed to sharpen so that she was aware of something she had not noticed before. There were flowers on a branch of the gorse bush beside her, tiny flowers of bright yellow, perching like minute butterflies on the snow crusting the branch. And that was strange, wasn't it, because summer was the time for gorse to bloom.

"Well?" With her voice coming out on a higher than usual note, she repeated her question.

Rhona looked up slowly, and said again, "Your mammy sent me to fetch you." She hesitated, looking at the others as if for support. Both Alec and Charlie kept their eyes on the ground, and Rhona finished in a rush, "Because he's dead. Granda McPhie's dead."

Now Charlie and Alec did look up; and now both of them did speak, their words mingling with one another.

"Half an hour ago, Cat. Grooming one of the ponies. Just dropped down dead in the snow. Your daddy picked him up. Your daddy said – "

Their voices went babbling on, but Cat did not hear what they said. The voices were voices no longer. They were just sounds beating around her head, beating like so many frantic bird wings. She spoke through the sounds, in tones that she seemed to hear like the voice of some stranger, coming to her from a distance.

"I'd better get back. I must get back."

She started running, letting the stones that were to have been her treasure trove drop, disregarded, from her loosened hold on her skirt. The other three ran with her, with Shuffler prancing alongside them as joyfully as if this, too, were just another of that morning's games in the cuckoo snow.

2

By the evening of that day, which was when they tracked her down to the camp, Cat had forgotten all about her brush with the police. How could you remember such a thing, after all, with your Daddy and Mammy roaring and crying all day for Granda McPhie, and your uncles and aunts and all your cousins, too, weeping their eyes out for him?

Cat struggled against the tide of grief, the terrible grief that always swept over her people at the death of any member of their close-knit families. But soon, like the rest of the children there, she was overwhelmed by it; and by the time they were all gathered around the camp fire that evening, her face was as swollen and tear-distorted as were those of the rest.

Then came the policemen, striding through the wood from the place where they had parked their car, two big heavy figures crashing their way through the undergrowth towards the travellers crouching by the fire.

Cat fled their approach, bolting like a rabbit for the safety of her family's tent. Her cousin Rhona followed her line of flight; and all the other children, too, were affected by her alarm. They scattered for the cover of tents and trailers, and peered out from this cover in fright that was now mingled with curiosity to see what would happen next.

Cat clutched Rhona and told her shakily, "I'm feared,

Rhona. Them's the very polis I ran from this mornin'."

"Hush, Cat, hush!" Rhona was not nearly so frightened as Cat. Besides, she was more than eight months the older of the two, and so there was authority in her voice. Cat felt less of shivering terror than before, and Rhona patted her approvingly. "That's right," she said. "Just keep still, Cat, and *listen*."

The sergeant was now standing by the fire, hands on hips, feet planted well apart. One pace behind him, the constable had taken up a more modest stance.

"You're getting out," the sergeant stated. "You're moving on from here, my buckos."

Andy McPhie rose slowly from between his brothers, Jim and George McPhie. "Big Andy" he was called, and in the normal way of things at least, he could have matched the sergeant for size. Big Andy also had a reputation as a fighter. But now, in the torpor of his grief, his heavy shoulders were slumped. All the aggression that was naturally his had drained out of him. But even so, he was still the eldest of the McPhie men, which meant he still had a duty to speak up for his brothers and his newly-widowed mother, Old Nan McPhie. Hoarsely he asked:

"What're you saying, sergeant? Why should we move?"

"Because I bloody well tell you to – that's why. Because you're the same kind of nuisance around here as you are everywhere else."

"Hold on there!" Now it was Daddler Drummond joining in, the contempt in the sergeant's voice making him spring up with the speed of a jack-in-the-box. And Daddler too – even more than Big Andy – was a fighter. "We're not on private land. What's more, this

13

wood's been a winter camp for travellers since – since – "
At a loss for the words he wanted, Daddler made a
clawing gesture as if he could drag them to him out of the
air; and it was the widow, Old Nan McPhie, who had
eventually to supply them.

"Since time immemorial."

The phrase was traditionally one from the Scottish
Highlands. The voice that spoke it had the singsong tones
of the Highlands. The sergeant, his eyes becoming
accustomed to the flicker of light and shadow created by
the fire, peered more closely at the travellers' faces. A
look of recognition began to dawn in his own face; and
briskly he told them:

"All right, then, let's have you. Who's all here?"

Sullenly they glanced at one another. Slowly, recog-
nising the inevitable, they gave their names – the three
McPhie brothers with their wives, Daddler and Maggie
Drummond, Hamish and Lorna MacDonald.

"Aye. Aye." The sergeant noted down the information
and gave a satisfied nod. "You do well to be honest with
your names, at least." Elaborately he returned the
notebook to his pocket. "And now, just tell me how
you're all related to one another. Because fine I know
that's always the way of it with you traveller families."

Sullenly again the travellers admitted to the network of
relationships between them. Maggie Drummond was the
sister of Andy McPhie's wife, Jean. Lorna MacDonald
was the sister of Jim McPhie's wife, Ilsa. George
McPhie's wife, Lizzie, had a brother-in-law who came
from the same family as Maggie Drummond and Jean
McPhie.

"Though it beats me," Daddler Drummond said, "what
all that's got to do with you!"

His hands were curling into fists as he spoke, and the tight smile on the sergeant's face showed that this had not escaped his notice.

"I'd be careful of those fists if I was you," he advised softly. "Those 'daddles' of yours. Because that's where you got your name, wasn't it? You, the fighter, the hard man that's always challenging 'put your daddles up.' And that's what it's got to do with me, you see. Because I've been lied to today already, over a tinker's name. But this – this wee interrogation, you might call it – is doing more than prove me right in my guess at what that name really was. It's helping me to remember where I've heard of you before – some of you, at least. Or where I've seen you before."

A pointing finger shot out at Jim McPhie, the youngest of the three brothers. "You, for instance. You're another one I remember. I've had you up in front of the Sheriff for poaching. Six years ago, that was; and 'Poacher' McPhie is what they call you."

The pointing finger swung round to Andy McPhie. "And you! You're the horse dealer among this little lot. And from all I've heard, you've pulled some fast tricks with some of the beasts you've sold."

"All right, all right, sergeant." Big Andy had been shaken out of his grief-induced torpor, and he spoke now more sharply than before. "But you can't blame us for anything this time around. All I've done these past winter months was to clear a bit of forest for firewood to sell. And I had a permit for that, too."

"Aye, from the Forestry Commission," George McPhie chimed in. "I know, sergeant, because I've been helping Andy with the wood. But that's all *I've* done."

"I've been dealing in car spares." Reluctantly, as the

15

sergeant glared down his truculent look, Daddler Drummond gave the information. "And what's more, I've lived as peaceable as the next man."

"I haven't had much work this winter," Hamish MacDonald admitted. "A bit of fencing here, a bit of ditching there, that's all. But nothing against the law, sergeant, that's for sure."

"I've been making willow baskets to sell when we take to the road again." Quietly, without raising his tear-swollen face, Jim McPhie came in at the tail end of the recital; and still with that tight, mirthless smile on his face, the sergeant asked the other policeman:

"Did you hear that, Constable Miller? Did you hear all those innocent lambs bleating away there? And not a one of them saying a word about sending his kid out to steal – eh? Oh, no, not a word about that!"

"No, sergeant, but – " The constable's eyes had been busy during the time he had been forced to stand in silence, and he had spotted Cat peering from the family tent. "There she is now."

All the faces around the fire swung to look at Cat. Then, slowly, Big Andy and Daddler sank back to their crouching position by the fire. If young Catriona McPhie was the cause of this visit from the police, it wasn't their place to sort out the trouble. Poacher would have to do that. Cat was the Poacher's girl.

"Come here, lassie." Poacher Jim was on his feet by this time, softly calling to her; and reluctantly loosing her clutch on Rhona, she came to him. "Now," with an arm around her shoulders, he encouraged her. "Speak to your Daddy, hen. What's up?"

Cat hung her head. "Nothin'. I never did nothin'."

"You wee liar!" Indignantly the words came shooting

out of the constable; but the sergeant waved him to silence and gave his own answer to Jim's question.

"I'll tell you what's up. She's been stealing eggs from the pheasant pens, up-bye on the estate. We caught her at it this morning, and – "

"I didn't, I didn't!" Vehemently Cat broke into the sergeant's words. "I never stole any eggs. I just looked into the pens with the birds in them. Honest, Daddy – " Desperately Cat tugged at her father's jacket, as desperately as if the very force of the action would show she was telling the truth. "The birds was so bonny I just stayed there lookin' at them, but that's all I did – honest to God, Daddy, that's all!"

"Shush, shush, I believe you." With both of his hands covering her frantic ones, her father calmed the babble of denial; but the sergeant's voice sounded above this reassurance.

"I tell you, McPhie, we caught her red-handed. And don't you tell me that a kid of her age would have been robbing pheasant pens unless you or some other scallywag like you had put her up to the trick – one that she's played often enough before, too, to judge from the complaint I got from the gamekeeper. And *that's* why I'm clearing you out of here, the whole shebang of you, lock stock and barrel – because that's the only way to deal with your thieving kind."

"But I never, I never, I never stole the eggs!" Once again Cat began shouting her denial, and a chorus of other voices joined with hers.

"And she wasn't put up to anything like that, either."
"It's no' fair!" "Damned polis aye houndin' us!"

The constable scowled at the swelling noise of protest. The sergeant's voice thundered through it.

17

"I'll give you 'damned polis'! Pheasant eggs is nobody's breakfast. Pheasant is game for gentry to shoot. Pheasant eggs is *valuable!* It's you that knows that, and it's me that won't have a parcel of thieving tinks on the very doorstep of a shooting estate. You'll be out of here by tomorrow's morn, or my name isn't Sergeant Murdo McKendrick!"

"And what if we're not?" With the force of Cat's denials ringing freshly in his mind, Jim McPhie felt bold enough to put the challenge, and grimly the sergeant accepted it.

"If you're not, my bucko, it'll be jail again for you. And as for your brat, she'll be put in a Home, where they'll maybe manage to knock some of the tinker ways out of her."

There was a brief, shocked silence, broken finally by a whimper of dismay from Cat. Her father took a firm grip of her. In a flat, toneless voice, knowing that he was now speaking for all the travellers there, he said:

"All right, we'll get out. But you'll have to give us time, first, to bury our dead."

"Dead?" The sergeant stared, like one suspecting himself the victim of a joke. "Who's dead?"

"My daddy." Jim McPhie choked over the grief that rose again in his throat, even while he spoke the words; but the constable knew so little of traveller ways that he tittered with laughter at the idea of a grown man calling his father "daddy".

"Cut that out, Miller!" Unexpectedly, the sergeant's anger was turned on the constable. The man fell into surly silence. The sergeant continued his questioning.

"Is this another of your tinker tricks, McPhie? Because, if it is . . . "

Jim spoke quietly into the threat left hanging in the air

18

between them. "Don't take my word for it sergeant. Ask at the undertaker's. They'll tell you old Andrew McPhie is dead."

The sergeant's face took on an oddly closed, blank look. Abruptly he said, "All right. I'll give you another forty-eight hours. And then that's it. That's final. We're not going to have your sort around here any longer. You see the old man off, and then you clear out. And as for that brat of yours, she'd better be thankful for small mercies – that's all I can say."

With a beckoning gesture to the constable, he turned away; but the two men had taken only a few steps from the fire when the sergeant halted to speak again.

"Your daddy – what did he die of?"

Jim McPhie looked down towards his mother, Old Nan; and in the eyes upturned to meet his gaze, he read the thoughts that were running through his own mind. Old Andrew McPhie hadn't been so old. Fifty-four was all the age he could have claimed; but that had been fifty-four years of travelling the roads in wet as well as shine, fifty-four years of being harassed from pillar to post by big voices from big men in blue uniforms – men like this one, who seemed to know so much about travellers but still *understood* nothing at all about them.

"I'm waiting, McPhie. What'd he die of?" The sergeant's reminder of his question broke the long gaze between son and widowed mother; but sharply as the man had spoken, Jim McPhie still took his time about answering. Drawing Cat with him, he settled back into crouching by the fire before he said:

"You could say, sergeant, that his heart gave out. Or if you wanted to put that another way – " He stopped, his eyes meeting those of his mother again before they went back to the looming figure of the sergeant.

"You could say," he finished, "that my daddy died of just being a traveller."

"Oh, hell!" said the sergeant. And then again, in the same abrupt and unexpected tone of regret, "Oh, hell!" All the travellers looked in amazement at him, but it was on the faces of the three McPhie brothers that the sergeant's gaze rested.

"Listen," he said, "I knew your daddy before any of you were born. *She'll* maybe remember that." Briefly he nodded to Old Nan. "The old woman, maybe she'll remember. I was a young bobby, just new on the Force. He was only a few years older than me. And he was a craftsman, a skilled tinsmith. He didn't have to wander the roads till his heart gave out. He could have settled down decently, with a steady job. He was a good man, quiet, a hard worker. Any boss would have taken him on. But no, he wouldn't have that. He wouldn't, he said, let anyone 'tie a label' on him."

Nobody spoke. No-one answered the sergeant's tirade. His gaze shifted to roam over the other faces around the fire, and beyond the fire to the tents and trailers, the ponies tethered to trees, the dogs lying nose on paws, the children peering firewards.

"You've got no sense," he said at last. "None of you has any more sense than poor old Andrew McPhie had. You won't even try to get settled work. We're in the 1970's, for God's sake, and still you're going on living the way he did — shiftless, rootless, like vagabonds from the Dark Ages."

The bulbous blue eyes rested momentarily on Cat. "As for this little tyke, you won't even blame her for the trouble she's brought on you, never mind give her the

20

sore backside she deserves. Because you don't believe in punishing bairns, do you? *She'll learn by doing*. That's all you'll ever say about this night's work! Nothing about the bother she's been to the estate, *and* to me. That won't mean anything at all to you, of course, because all you care about is yourselves and your families. Other people don't mean a brass farthing to you – do they? But they do to me. It's my job to care about all those decent, honest, settled folk. And so it's no wonder, is it, that you're such a thorn in my flesh?"

The travellers stared into the fire, once again making silence their only response. The sergeant shrugged. The lines of his face tightened till it was as hard as it had been before the mention of Andrew McPhie's death.

"All right." With swift renewal of anger in his voice, he gave them his final word. "Forty-eight hours, remember, and then you're out. That's what I said. And, by God, you'd better believe me, that's what I still mean!"

3

Granda McPhie's trailer had been burnt to ashes according to the tradition which said that a dead man's trailer – or his tent – always had to be burned, and Old Nan McPhie had announced her decision to travel thenceforth with her youngest son, Jim, his wife Ilsa, and their daughter, Cat. The families had dispersed to go their separate ways. At Old Nan's wish, Jim's lot had headed north with the old lady herself sitting all hunched up with her grief in the cart drawn by the grey pony, Pibroch. And Cat, for one, was glad to have left the camp behind her.

It was true, of course, that no-one had blamed her for the way it had been broken up. The sergeant had been right in that, at least. But there had still been something frightening in the sight of Granda's trailer going up in flames. And she had liked it even less when the whisky flowed as they mourned him, with Daddler Drummond getting so drunk at last that he had quarrelled with Maggie Drummond, and the quarrel had finished up with him giving her a terrible beating.

Poor Maggie! And poor Charlie Drummond, too. Charlie had cried and begged the other men to stop his Daddy paggerin' his Mammy, but even his big brothers wouldn't do that for him. You couldn't interfere between husband and wife, they had all said, and – white as a sheet by that time – Charlie had vowed:

"I'll kill him for this. I swear it! Before God I swear, some day I'll kill my Daddy!"

Cat pushed away the thought of the white distress that had prompted the words. The sun was shining, the cuckoo snow all gone. It was great to be on the road again, walking along like this in her usual place at the tail of the cart. And drink, thank God, wasn't a curse with her Daddy the way it was with so many other travelling men, so that she would never have to watch her Mammy take a beating the way it had been with Maggie. Besides, it was very likely she would meet up with Charlie again at the old traveller site just north of Perth. Daddler Drummond had said he would take his lot that way so that he could have some dealings in scrap metal with a merchant in the town; and she could see how Charlie was feeling then – maybe even ask him if he really meant to keep that terrible vow he'd made.

Her step grew buoyant. There was Spring green thrusting out all round her, birds soaring overhead, and she was as free now as they were – nobody to tell her what to do, no rules to bother her; because the winter camp, of course, had taken care of the hundred days' schooling a year that the law demanded of traveller children. She began to whistle. Shuffler pranced a little in sympathy with the high spirits he sensed in her. Her father's brown lurcher, Sheba, pricked an ear to the sound. She grinned down at both of them, and knew she was going to enjoy every minute of the time it would take to reach the camp north of Perth.

It was through farmland their way led; and Jim foresaw plenty of occasions where his skill at willow-work meant he could pick up wages for mending baskets and other gear needed for the work of the year ahead. Besides which, the road ran alongside a river that he reckoned was a good trout-water.

"I could take many a fine fish out of there," he remarked; and Old Nan was sufficiently roused to nod in reply before she warned him:

"Aye. But not before you're out of that sergeant's bailiwick."

Ilsa also nodded agreement with his remark – a silent nod, and rather a vague one compared to Old Nan's emphatic gesture. But that, thought Cat, was her Mammy's style. There was always a faraway air about her and she never had much to say for herself – except, of course, when it came to any kind of selling or trading; and then she could be brisk and glib enough! As if she had read this last thought, Ilsa looked back at Cat and said quietly:

"There's a place ahead where we can start selling your Daddy's baskets."

And that, Cat told herself, was another thing about her Mammy. She had a way of being able to tell what you were thinking even before you could find words to say it to yourself. And more! She could see into the future – really see, so that she knew what would happen to people. Her Mammy was one of those that had 'the gift'!

The approach to the houses Ilsa had in mind was by means of a path leading up through a plantation of young birch trees that covered the rising ground on the side of the road opposite to the river. Jim halted Pibroch at the foot of the path, and then unhooked some of the baskets that hung around the cart. Ilsa and Cat each took a sack from among the gear in the cart. Jim looped the baskets together so that they made two separate lots, gave one of these to Ilsa, the other to Cat, and told them both:

"Off you go, then. But remember, when God made time He made plenty of it, so there's no rush to get back to me and the old one. We'll just smoke a quiet pipe together till we see you again."

He turned his head towards Old Nan, smiling, his look inviting an answering smile in the thought of the small pleasure ahead; but Old Nan had retreated into the gloom that had held her almost constantly since her husband's death. Ilsa shook her head in sympathy with this setback to Jim's hopes, then stepped towards the path. Cat went with her, a small and very sturdy figure by contrast with her mother's slender, light-stepping grace. One behind the other, then, they climbed the path between the thin silver and the delicately-shivering new green of the young birches; and as they neared the end of the climb, Ilsa said:

"You've not seen this place before, Cat, but I have. There's a row of cottages we can try first – up there, see?" She pointed to the gable end of the row, just coming into sight at the top of the slope. "We'll see what the wifies there have to say."

The cottages were of the kind usually occupied by farm workers and their like – in traveller terms, 'the country hantle.' Their roofs were of grey-blue slate, their low walls of stone inset with windows too small to allow much light to enter. Cat knew them well, and equally well she knew the varied forms of reception she might get from the women who lived in them.

Some of these women would be hostile to her or any traveller, from others she might get a grudging sort of tolerance. If the woman was young enough to have children of her own, it was a fair bet that this would make her more likely to show sympathy to a traveller child. But hostile or tolerant, kind or uncaring, most of them would still be wary of her and her Mammy. Afraid of the day they never saw, she thought contemptuously. That was always the way of things with these settled people. She watched her mother knock at the door of the first house, and saw the door open to show a middle-aged face with a frown of suspicion on it.

"It's a grand day, Missis . . . " Smoothly Ilsa launched into the flow of pleasantries that might hold the woman long enough for her to be interested in the baskets. Always be the first to start talking, and keep your talk flowing so easy and polite that the other woman couldn't get a word in edgeways. That was the important thing to remember – but the woman's frown had deepened. In the small, dim hallway behind her, there was no sign of children. And she didn't want to buy a basket.

"Not from you tinks anyway," she said, reaching a hand to close the door as she spoke. But Cat's quick glance around the hallway had caught an opened sack of potatoes pushed back into a corner; and the woman's husband, she reckoned, would be a farm hand who had got those tatties free, as one of the perks of his job. Quickly she slid her left foot forward so that the door jammed on it, and put on a whining voice.

"If you could just spare a boiling of tatties then, Missis. I'm that hungry! Even one tattie . . . "

"Oh, you, you – " The woman was furiously pushing the door against her foot, but Cat kept up her whining pleas, even although she was now inwardly laughing at the way annoyance had suddenly made the woman a ridiculous figure – face red-flushed, hair falling wispily forward, mouth working in a useless effort to obey the anger in her brain.

"One tattie wouldn't hurt, Missis, would it? Just one, eh?"

"Oh, for God's sake!" The woman whirled to the sack, scooped some potatoes from it, and thrust them at Cat. She grabbed them as they fell away from the woman's hands, and turned away. The door banged shut. Ilsa spoke from the corner of her mouth as she led the way down the path.

"Don't laugh. If she sees you laughing she might set the polis on us."

With an effort Cat suppressed the laugh rising in her. Everything a traveller girl had to learn about hawking baskets or any other traveller woman's work, she learned from her mother; and so always, on these occasions, it was a case of *Do as your Mammy tells you.*

At the foot of the path, it was Ilsa who was the first to smile. 'Serve that mean old besom right," she said, 'you cadging the tatties off her. Not that there's enough to make a boiling for us, of course; but it's a start, lassie. It's still a start in the right direction."

Cat put the potatoes in her sack, smiling at this praise, and they went up the path to the second house.

The woman there was young. A gaggle of small children clung to her skirts, underfed-looking children, with runny noses and red-rimmed eyes. As if they all had colds, Cat thought. They were poorly-dressed too, and she could feel her heart rising in indignant compassion for them. The woman herself was pale and thin. She had a defeated air about her – too much so for any of the usual wariness of travellers to appear. And yes, she said, she would have liked a nice willow basket, but money was short and the children needed clothes, and so – Her head drooped. She gave a helpless wave of her hands.

"I'll tell you what," Ilsa said. "You just take a basket for free – to cheer you up, like, eh? And I'll get you

27

clothes for the wee ones – good stuff, too, and I'll sell it to you cheaper than you'd buy in any shop. Here, lass!" She bent to the smallest of the children and looped a basket over her skinny little arm. "You take that for your Mammy." She straightened up. "And we'll be back, Missis."

They left the young woman gaping after them and went on to the next house, with Cat asking her mother:

"Where you goin' to get the clothes, then?"

"At the laird's house," Ilsa told her, "about half a mile from here. I mind that the woman there has bairns about the same age as the ones belonging that poor young soul."

The rest of the houses in the row provided a mixed haul. They sold two baskets. They traded another three for some flour, more potatoes, and a largish lump of cheese. At the last house, the woman threatened to set her dog on them. Calmly, Ilsa told her:

"Don't be daft, Missis. When did you ever see a traveller that couldn't deal with a dog?"

They left the woman staring after them, and walked till they found a grassy hollow where they could sit down to eat the cheese.

"But only half of it, remember," Ilsa cautioned. "We must still leave a good bite for your Daddy and your Nan."

The cheese was yellow, and crumbly, and richly-flavoured. Cat was still revolving the taste of it in her mouth when they reached the entrance to the driveway of the laird's house; but all further thought of it vanished when Ilsa said to her:

"Well, there you are, Cat. On you go. And mind, it's not the cook or the nanny or such-like that you want to talk to. It's herself – the woman of the house."

"Me?" Cat gaped at her mother. "On my own?"

"It'll be good practice for you. In there is gentry — the 'bene hantle.' And it's time, isn't it, that you learned to deal with them on your own instead of always having your Mammy to talk for you?"

"Aye, well . . . " Cat drew a deep breath and studied the prospect before her. The driveway was long and curving. The house at the end of the drive was the biggest she had ever seen — a massive pile of grey stone, tall-windowed, and with a wide sweep of stone steps leading up to its main door. Ilsa pointed to the evidence of children's play on the lawn in front of the house — the tricycle, the big, coloured ball, the swing attached to the lowest branch of the big tree at the centre of the lawn.

"And Cat," she said, "one last thing. Do your best — will you? — to get the right sizes for that poor woman's bairns."

"I will, Mammy." Cat took another deep breath and started out along the driveway. Almost at once, then, she felt the enclosing warmth created by the shelter of the thick rhododendron hedge cast in a semi-circle around the lawn on her left, and growing high also on the right-hand side of the drive. Among the scattered toys on the smooth green of the lawn itself was a set of white-painted garden chairs and a white table. The rhododendrons were alive with the sound and movement of small birds. From somewhere behind the house came fainter indications of noise and action — voices laughing, and the occasional tell-tale sounds of a tennis match being played. But it was still primarily the house that held Cat's attention. Because how, she wondered, how in the name of creation was she going to get speech with the mistress of a pile like that?

Cautiously she rounded a corner of the place, eyes

29

questing for a kitchen entrance, and realised immediately that this was her lucky day. It had to be, she thought, because here she suddenly was in a sort of courtyard, and there in front of her was a baby asleep in its pram, with a uniformed nanny holding on to the pram's handle. And beside the pram was a youngish woman in another kind of uniform – the cashmere, and tweed, and pearls that were always the marks of the bene hantle! Besides which – to judge by the way she was fussing over the baby, at least – this other woman was its mammy, the mistress of the big house, no less! With a nod of greeting to both women, Cat launched into her usual stream of polite and easy talk.

The nanny and the bene hantle woman stared at her, then at one another. The bene hantle woman's eyes came back to Cat. Impatiently she cut across the talk.

"Yes, yes, but what is it you *want?*"

Quickly, her voice as bossy as her manner, the nanny chimed in. "Don't speak to her, m'lady, or she'll just try to take advantage of you. She's a *tinker!*"

The bene hantle woman's puzzled look changed suddenly to one of cold and haughty displeasure. "Thank you, Nanny," she said in a voice that was the very opposite of thanks. "I'll make my own decisions."

The nanny went scarlet in the face. Nanny, Cat told herself, had put her foot in it. And by the sound of things, it wasn't the first time that had happened! Quick as light she pressed home the advantage the scene had given her.

"It's my wee brothers and sisters, Missis," she said humbly. "In rags, they are, hardly a stitch to their backs, and my poor Mammy crying and lamenting 'Are the bairns to go naked, God help us, and rich folk maybe with clothes they don't need for their own bairns.' And so, if you could just let me have a coat here, or a wee dress there – just the things your own bairns have no use for now, of course – it would be a blessing, Missis. And it's not that I'm asking something for nothing, either. Because see here, I have baskets to trade – "

The woman had stopped listening, Cat realised, but she was thinking instead. You could tell that from the way she was pursing her lips and sliding her eyes sideways for an occasional look at the nanny. But it was just as well to go on talking, of course – not to mention keeping an eye on that nanny! Just in case . . .

"What ages are your – er – your brothers and sisters?" The bene hantle lady seemed to have made up her mind. Her question cut across Cat's renewed flow of talk; and quickly she responded, inventing names as she went along.

"Jamie, Missis, he's seven. Rob's six; and the twins, wee Alice and Jean, are just four."

"Nanny – ." The bene hantle woman turned and spoke rapidly in an undertone. The nanny listened, her face 'as sour as curdled milk', Cat thought gleefully. But Nanny had to watch out for her job, and there was no more word about tinkers before she disappeared into the house. The bene hantle woman studied Cat, her eyes coming to rest distastefully on the sack draped over her back. Cat stood in silence, ignoring the look, her mind busy instead with the triumphant thought of the clothes she would get on the nanny's return. Half an hour from now, she told herself, and her Mammy would be pocketing the money for these clothes. *And* her Mammy would have sold them to that other woman at a price the poor creature could afford!

"Your baskets," the bene hantle woman said suddenly. "Who made them?"

Cat smiled at her, pleased by the question. "My Daddy," she said proudly. "He's real good at the willow work. Here!" She held out a basket. "You can have this. I said I'd trade for the clothes."

The woman took a step back, drawing the pram with her. "Er – thank you, no. It's – um – very nice, but you might – um – that is, I don't want the baby to catch anything."

The retort that sprang to Cat's mind was a sharp one. *If he catches anything it'll no' be from me. It'll be a stiff neck from you!* But it would be stupid, she warned herself, to offend the bene hantle by saying that. And if there was one thing travellers couldn't afford to be, it was stupid! She bit her lip on the retort, and in silence again, the two of them waited till the nanny returned with a bundle of children's clothes in her arms.

Disdainfully she thrust the clothes forward; and joyfully Cat examined them. Fine serge, wool, linen – every garment was as good as she had expected it to be. Beautiful stuff, she thought; just beautiful. It didn't need the posh makers' labels inside to tell you the quality of this lot! And all in sizes that would just fit the other woman's bairns! With thanks pouring out of her, she backed away with the bundle, and turned to hurry away down the drive to her mother.

The tennis players whose presence she had guessed at earlier had seemingly taken a break from their game. They were sitting sprawled on the white chairs on the lawn, a group of leggy fifteen and sixteen year olds sipping drinks from a tray of tall glasses set on the white table. They stared at her approach along the driveway, turned to speak to one another, and stared again as she drew level with them, laughing this time as they stared.

Cat hurried past, not realising at all the odd picture she presented – baskets over one arm, bundle clutched to her chest, the sack that hung over one shoulder drooping below her short dress and bumping jerkily against her sturdy, childish legs. The mockery in the laughter, however, was more than plain to her; and towards the end of the drive she stopped to look back at the young tennis-players.

They thought they were so clever, she told herself, with their fancy clothes and nothing to do but sit in a sheltered garden drinking fancy drinks. But they'd laugh on the other side of their faces if they knew how travellers sharpened up their wits on people like them!

A large contempt for the tennis players filled her mind. It was just as well for them, she thought, that *they* could afford to be stupid, because there wasn't a traveller born who couldn't make rings round them! As for their house, that grand mansion of theirs, what was that anyway but a sort of prison just like any other house? That's where they would sleep that night, in a great heavy-roofed prison of stone walls, while she would still be as free as the birds of the air – free as the very air itself!

On impulse she allowed her clutter of baskets and bundle to drop to the ground. The tennis players were still staring towards her. She could still hear their laughter, distanced now, but no less mocking. With great deliberation she raised her hands to her face and made the gesture of thumbing her nose at them. Then, just as deliberately, she picked up her burdens and continued jauntily on her way.

4

They had been three weeks on the road now, travelling
slow enough to let Ilsa and Cat continue hawking around
the doors, stopping altogether for a few days when Jim
found work on a farm. Old Nan's interest in life had
begun to revive and Cat had great hopes that she would
soon become again the story-telling Nan of past times.
Perhaps, she told herself, when they had fresh company
at the camp where she hoped to meet up with Charlie
Drummond; and looked eagerly ahead as they reached
the place.

The Drummonds were there, along with another
traveller family, the Reids. But Charlie wasn't among
them. Cat hung back from the flurry of greetings that
followed the arrival of her own family, with wariness of
meeting Morven Reid added to her disappointment at not
seeing Charlie. Joe Reid she knew. Joe was Maggie
Drummond's brother. And Joe's wife, Morven, was sister
to her own Uncle George's wife, Lizzie; but even so,
Morven was still a stranger to her, because Morven and
Lizzie came of an Irish travelling family and Joe Reid had
travelled mostly in Ireland since he and Morven had
married.

"And what's brought us across, you ask?" That was
Morven Reid speaking now, tossing her head of fine black
hair on the words and glinting her eyes provocatively
sideways at the men in the group. "A longin' on me,

34

that's what did it; the longin' sometimes to see my sister Lizzie, that's married on Jim's own brother. And of course, the chance to meet with such grand fellows as the Daddler, here. And yourself too, Jim."

Jim and Daddler both laughed at this. Maggie Drummond looked sour. Ilsa's face went blank and quiet. Joe Reid said hastily:

"Now, Morven, you know it's more than the chance of visiting that's brought us across. Show them all what's in there."

He jerked his head towards the Reid trailer, and everyone crowded to its door. Just inside the door stood something carefully covered by a piece of sacking. Morven whipped off the sacking, and stood proudly displaying a piece of antique furniture – a small, bow-fronted chest of drawers, with delicate stringing inset along the curving front of each drawer.

" 'Tis good money I'll get for this over here," she told them, and ran loving hands across surfaces that had the sheen of satin on them. "A lot more than it would fetch on the other side of the water."

A mutter of agreement rose from the other travellers. From Ilsa and Maggie, now, came looks of respectful envy. It was amazing, of course, the things you could stumble across when you were going about the doors; amazing too, how you could beat down the price when you were dealing with people who didn't know how to bargain. And many a good antique had fallen cheaply into their own hands. But this find of Morven's, their eyes told one another, certainly surpassed any that they had ever made.

Moura, the second oldest of the Reid children and the only girl among them, pushed forward to say pertly:

"And 'tis myself will get some of the money, because my Mammy promised it to me to buy gold earrings to set off my good looks."

Once again there was laughter from the men – this time with Joe Reid included. Moura had the same black hair as Morven, and obviously the same conceit of her appearance. Young as she was, too – about twelve, Cat guessed – she had given the same coquettish toss of the head, the same provocative glint of the eyes. And now she was looking for something to prolong the moment of preening herself on the men's laughter. Her glance came to rest on the small hoops of gold wire in Cat's ears; and pointedly she added:

"Big earrings!"

Hurriedly Cat backed out of the group. Those earrings had been her cousin Rhona's gift to her at the traditional present-sharing just before the break-up of the winter camp. And Rhona was her best friend, as well as being her cousin. *Anything* that Rhona gave her was precious; and so she certainly wasn't going to stand there and let that Moura creature make mock of her little earrings!

There was a wood beyond the stream that ran past the camp. She headed for the wood with Shuffler, as usual, bounding along behind her, and found herself running alongside the river that the stream had joined. The wood was quiet, no sound there except the dull thud of her own running steps. But the path was a winding one that closely followed the river's course, and there were tree roots sprawled across it. Eyes down to the hazards it presented she began to forget her anger and to run, instead, simply for the joy of running.

The river bank broadened. The path ended abruptly where the bank was indented by a pebbly bay, and the sudden appearance there of girl and dog startled a group of swans that had been sailing close inshore. The swans burst into flight, wings filling the air with a white whirl of panic; and Cat was brought up dead in her tracks, staring in enchantment at the sight of that winged explosion.

Shuffler, after his first reaction of alarm, ignored the swans; but Cat held her place, still feasting her eyes on them. They circled, long necks outstretched, wing beats steadied to an even, powerful stroke, then turned away from the river to fly over the wood and finally out of sight. Yet still Cat stayed where she was; and still her mind was filled by the wild white beauty of that first explosion into flight.

"Aye, Cat!" A voice from behind her startled her out of her trance. She turned quickly, and saw Charlie Drummond standing a few feet from where the path ran into the bay.

"Charlie!" In the pleased surprise of the moment, Cat found herself blundering into a confused version of the question she had meant to put so carefully to him. "I was wondering, Charlie – I mean, are you all right now? Because of that business about your Mammy, you see, and you being so upset and all."

"I'm all right." Charlie spoke with some awkwardness in his manner; but he hadn't seemed to mind her asking, and so she ventured again:

"And that vow you made, Charlie, that terrible thing you said about killing your Daddy some day – you wouldn't keep such a vow, would you?"

For a moment, Charlie looked even more awkward than before. He rumpled his shock of sandy-fair hair. His ruddy Drummond face took on a slightly deeper colour, and then slowly began to grin. Sheepishly, he said:

"Ach, you know me, Cat. I can't hold a grudge against anyone — never mind my own Daddy."

"Well," said Cat. "Well!" She gave a relieved smile in reply to his grin. "So you really are all right, then."

"I told you I was." Charlie leaned against a tree and began idly poking at the ground with the long stick of ashwood he carried in one hand. The stick was forked at one end. In his other hand was a largish tin jug that had a glass bottom. With one small part of her mind Cat noted that the stick and jug meant he was off to hunt for pearls in the mussel beds of the river; but the greater part of her mind was still occupied with the incident behind her questions, and after a moment, she said:

"I don't like it, all the same, the way traveller men take it for granted they can beat up their wives. I mean, it isn't fair, is it?"

"Maybe not." Charlie shrugged in a way that showed he was not keen to pursue the issue. "But it's the way things are. And you don't hear any of our folks shouting about it."

"I would!" Cat was quite positive on this point. "I'm damned if I'd let any man do that to me."

"How're you going to stop it?" The look that Charlie gave with this was a scornful one, and she stared in momentary confusion before she answered lamely:

"Oh, I'll think of something, I suppose." With a nod to the stick and the job, she did her best then to change the subject. "I see you're off to the pearling."

"I'll have a try at it, anyway. There's some good mussel beds in this river, and you never know your luck." Charlie began miming the business of pearl-fishing as he spoke, peering downwards through the glass bottom of the jug, and jabbing the forked end of his stick in the act

38

of lifting an imaginary mussel from the water. Cat smiled at the antics, and then spoke on impulse with not a thought in her head except the fact that the camp held no-one else near her own age – except for Moura Reid, of course, the girl she didn't want to know.

"Can I have a try too, Charlie? I don't mind wading deep in the water. And I know the right kind of mussels to fish for – the ones that grow crooked-shelled when the pearl starts to form inside them. I've opened thousands of those for my Daddy, and found pearls in them too. But I'd still like to be the one that does the fishing for them."

Charlie had stopped his fooling, and the face that had appeared from behind the jug was surprised at first, and then disapproving. Scornfully he asked:

"What d'you want to be, then? A split mechanic?"

Cat went red with embarrassment. She'd forgotten, of course. Traveller women and girls did only women's work – never anything like pearl-fishing. That was men's work; and "split mechanic" was always the sexual insult that male travellers used among themselves to describe a woman or a girl who practised any of a man's skills.

"I'm not," she said confusedly. "I mean, I don't want to – "

"Because if you are a split mechanic," Charlie interrupted her, grinning with teasing enjoyment of the way he had suddenly embarrassed her, "you'll never get married, will you? Not to any traveller man, at least."

"That's what you think!" Gamely Cat tried to defend herself, but the confidence she attempted sat uneasily on her. "And anyway – " She groped for inspiration, and came up with a retort that would surely crush Charlie.

"It'll be long years yet before *I* need to think of getting married."

Charlie grinned again at this, an even more teasing grin. "Just you ask your Old Nan about that," he advised. "She'll tell you different. I know she will too, because my Mammy told me that Old Nan had her first bairn before she was fourteen. And my Mammy had two before *she* was sixteen."

It was true, Cat thought glumly. Traveller girls did marry early. But all the same, she wasn't going to let Charlie Drummond brand her for a split mechanic who'd never get married – and all just because she'd wanted to have a try at the pearling. Her confusion hardened suddenly into an anger that was all the more intense because Charlie was supposed to be her friend.

"You've got a bad, dirty mouth, Charlie Drummond," she stormed. "And I'll tell my Daddy on you."

Charlie gaped in dismay at her expression, at the fierce tone that told him he had carried his teasing too far. "Och, Cat," he pleaded, and tried to grab her arms as she flung away from him. "I didn't mean it. Honest I didn't."

"Then don't say it!" Charlie had missed the attempted hold and she was shouting back at him as she ran along the path. "Don't say things you don't mean!"

She'd wasted her sympathy on him, she told herself furiously as she ran. And it was the last time she'd ever make *that* mistake. But there, as it happened, she had done Charlie an injustice; and because she was no more capable of holding anger than he was, she was glad when she discovered that to be so.

It was Morven Reid's teasing tongue, strangely enough, that healed the breach. Morven had her eye on the grey pony, Pibroch; and when they were all gathered around the fire that evening, she spoke her mind about it.

"Such a terrible broad back it has," she remarked. "I've never seen the like of such a creature!"

The mockery in the words was so clear that Cat felt an immediate sense of outrage. Pibroch was part of her life! Pibroch was the companion of all her days, the strong, steady presence she rewarded every evening with a sweet bite specially saved for him! She opened her mouth to speak, but Charlie was quicker off the mark than she was. Charlie had sometimes laughed at her over that sweet bite, but Charlie knew how fond she was of Pibroch!

"If you've never seen the like of Pibroch," he said, "it's because you've never before met with so special a breed as the hill garron."

"D'you tell me so!" Morven exclaimed, but the note of mockery was still in her voice. Charlie flushed to hear it, and looked at Jim McPhie as if to show that he knew it was really Jim's responsibility to take up the cudgels. But all that Jim did was to smile and give a wave of his pipe that indicated he was quite content to let Charlie finish what he had started. And Charlie, although he wasn't the talkative kind as a rule, was fluent enough when he wanted to be!

With the greatest of satisfaction Cat listened to him telling Morven all about the breed of hill garron – how strong it was, how that breadth of back was a special feature cultivated for centuries to give it its strength, how rare specimens of the breed were nowadays, and how lucky was the man who owned one.

"Good for you, Charlie," her father said when the recital was finished; but it was at her that Charlie looked, smiling a little, yet with an anxious expression in his eyes that seemed to beg her to accept the amends he had offered in springing to Pibroch's defence. She smiled in answer, a smile that told him how handsome she thought the amends and how gratefully she had accepted them. Then, with a pleasant feeling of relief in the knowledge that their quarrel was now dead and buried, she leaned back against the cushiony comfort of Old Nan and prepared to give her attention to the rest of the conversation.

" – and oh, the horses that are in it with us in Ireland!" Morven Reid was saying. "I mind me of the Puck Fair at Killorglin, in County Kerry, and the horses you'll see there. Beautiful, they are, just beautiful – great big hunters, all of them so tall and powerful, the legs of them goin' like pistons when they're brought out to show their paces, and every traveller in Ireland there to admire them! Ah, it's a great sight, I tell you, the horses at the Puck."

Moura Reid spoke, lifting up her dark head from its resting-place on her father's shoulder. "We go there every year, the whole family of us. And I mind me once, I saw a wee red filly for sale. Red as a strawberry she was, like silk to the touch, and the long legs of her stepping like she was a dancer on a stage. I'd have given my heart, so I would, for that wee red filly. And indeed, it's a princess I would have been, mounted on her."

Everyone was looking at Moura now, quite fascinated by the small story in her words – and not just because travellers always were fascinated by a story, Cat realised. It was Moura herself who held their attention, the picture Moura presented with her big dark eyes now so wistful, the finespun tendrils of her dark hair so delicately framing her high cheekbones. Cat thought of her own thick, straight hair, her own eyes of such nondescript hazel colour, and was sharply envious of Moura's beauty.

"Never mind, my hen." Joe Reid broke the silence, drawing Moura back to him as he spoke. "Filly or no wee red filly, you'll aye be my princess."

There was a little laugh at this. Joe went on talking, and Moura leaned her head on his shoulder again – although, Cat noticed, this was not before she had given them all a glance that showed her satisfaction with the impression she had made. But Joe's talk had brought the conversation round to plans for the immediate future; and now he was asking: "So where are you headed with your lot, Jim?"

"North," Jim told him; and Old Nan added:

"Aye, north to the hills of home."

The hills of home. But how could a traveller have a home? Puzzled by the contradiction in her grandmother's words, Cat twisted round to stare up into Old Nan's face. "I thought," she said, "that you'd always been a traveller."

"So I have, lassie. Been on the road all my life – like my Mammy and Daddy before me, and their Mammy and Daddy before them, 'way back to time immemorial."

"Then how can you have a home?"

"Because it makes no difference how far you travel, my hen, or how many years you spend on the road. There's always something that calls you back to some place that feels special to you – maybe because it's the place where it all started. And you can't be at peace till you see it again. That's 'home' for a traveller. Just being at peace in the one place where – for a while at least – you don't feel the need to journey."

"That's what it'll be like for me," Ilsa said, "when we get to a wee glen just west of Inverness. I'll not need to go as far north as you, Nan."

"No. But you'll still take me on to my enchanted land, you and Jim." Old Nan leaned forward to knock the ash out of her pipe. "Bless your hearts for that." She rose stiffly, with Cat helping her to her feet. "And now I'm for my bed."

"Me too!" Cat spoke quickly, her mind so full of the questions she had to ask that the fireside talk no longer held any attraction for her. *The place where it all started.* But why had it started? What had put them all on the road in the first place? The questions came tumbling out of her as she followed Old Nan into their tent; and with weary patience, the old woman explained:

"There was no one thing started it all. Travellers are just folk that have been put on the road for any one of a dozen different reasons – most of them to do with bad luck of some kind. And we get the name of 'tinkers' because some of them were tinsmiths – like your Granda McPhie – that made a living at the kind of pot-mending they call 'tinkling'.

"Like gypsies, Nan? The ones we sometimes see down south at St Boswells Fair? Because they're travellers, too, are they no'? And they mend pots?"

"Aye. But *we're* no' gypsies. They're a folk that came long ago from a far country; a folk that still has a language that's all their own. And we're just the homeless ones o' this land.'

Old Nan's weariness was getting the upper hand of her, and she yawned as she spoke. "But where they could settle again, these homeless ones, they did – except for a few hundred families like ourselves. And the reason that we never gave up the travelling life is that we have something different in our natures from the ones that did settle."

"But what's the something, Nan? What's different about us?"

"Oh, go to sleep, lassie." Creakily, Old Nan lowered herself on to the bundle of dry grass that Cat had cut to make a bed for them both. "If you're not tired talking, I am."

Cat lay down by her grandmother's side, reluctantly accepting that there would be no more information forthcoming that night. But with sleep still far from her, and her mind still busy with her final, unanswered question, she became restless for a last look at the night outside. She listened to the old woman's breathing. The tent in which the two of them lay was the traditional traveller tent – no more than a piece of canvas stretched over willow branches bent into half-hoops; and one of her hands, as she listened, crept out to grip a corner of the canvas. The old woman's breathing took on the rhythm of sleep; and with a twitch of the hand, Cat threw open her corner of the tent.

The stars sprang out at her as suddenly as the startled opening of countless huge and glittering eyes, and she felt a shiver of delight in such instant brilliance. It was just like the moment the swans had burst into flight, she thought. The swans had been an explosion of white. The stars were an explosion of silver.

Swans and stars, swans and stars . . . The words ran like a chant in her mind, and underneath the sound of them she could feel the unwinding of all her memories of the past weeks on the road. The free-as-a-bird sensation it gave to be all day in the open, the smoky taste of tea made with water boiled on the fire, the delight of pitting her wits against women who came surly to the door and gradually thawed under a flow of easy talk – Cat let the flap of canvas fall back into place, wondering as she did so how those women could bear to live such walled-up lives. Prisoners' lives! Lives where there would never be any moments of swans and stars!

Vaguely, too, as sleep began to take hold of her, she wondered again about the "something different" in her nature that set her apart from such people. And did the same also, of course, for other travellers. Because they all had that something different in them, those who weren't her kin, as well as those who were; her friends too, Rhona, and Alec, and Charlie –

Charlie . . . There had been plenty of fights before among herself and the other three, but they had always made up again; and she was certainly glad to have made up, this time, with Charlie. *Charlie* . . .

A voice sounded in the drowsy cavern of her mind, her own voice, yet still one that was strangely unlike the one she had then. The voice was speaking to Charlie – not the thirteen year old Charlie she knew, but a different, older Charlie with an expression of sullen exasperation on his face. And this voice that was her own yet still eerily not her own, was telling him loudly, in angry and decisive tones:

All right, if you want it straight. Your Daddy's a drunk, and I won't share my life with a drunk. I'll never travel with your family, Charlie.

5

The lush farm lands of Perthshire dropped behind them, and Ilsa spoke encouragingly to Cat about the next stage in the journey north.

"The worst bit of our road now, my hen, will be the Pass of Drumochter. If this fine weather holds till we're through the Pass, there's nothing else to worry about."

The weather held through days of blazing June sunshine that lightened even the dark conifers climbing the steep, rocky crags on either side of the road. They came out into its full glow in a stretch of moor and field with tiny villages strung out along their way, and then passed through a small town thronged with summer tourists.

Tourists and natives alike eyed them strangely as they passed; but they were used, by this time, to such looks. The road was the main route to the north, and there were always holiday-makers rushing past in their cars, with passengers pointing out to one another the unusual sight of travelling people who were still old-fashioned enough to use a pony and cart. They stopped in a layby for a drink of cold tea, and several cars pulled into the same layby. People got out of the cars to photograph them sitting on the road verge, and Ilsa said satirically:

"We should get the Tourist Board to sell tickets to see us."

"You're right," Jim agreed. "Roll up, roll up, ladies and

gents. Come and see a gen-ew-ine old-time tinker family. But here! I'll give them value for money, even without their tickets!"

He rose towards the cart and rummaged in it till he found his set of bagpipes. Old Nan smiled at Ilsa – the first time any of them had seen her smile since the death of Granda McPhie – and Ilsa smiled in reply. Jim was terrible on the pipes. They both knew that, and so did he. But what did that matter? the exchange of smiles asked. A tinker piper playing at the roadside was one of the traditions of the country, after all – which was just what these tourists had come to see! And the McPhies needed the money that even Jim's playing would coax out of them. Besides which, these people probably couldn't tell a drone from a chanter, anyway, or a chanter from a hole in the wall!

Jim had the bag filled now and was beginning to tune up. The pipes burst into full voice. Solemnly he marked time to the first few notes and then began to march up and down, tartan streamers flying from the drones, the pipes caterwauling at their loudest. The tune he had chosen made Old Nan and Ilsa exchange glances again. Their smiles turned to giggles; and Cat, as she also recognised the tune and remembered the bawdy words to it, was equally overcome with giggles.

One of the tourists – a woman with owlish-looking spectacles and an earnest expression to match – had taken a tape-recorder from her car and was recording the din. The other tourists took more photographs. Ilsa gave Cat a nudge that brought her scrambling to her feet. With the mug that had contained her tea held in one hand, she started going around the tourists, shaking the mug under their noses and chanting:

"Spare something for the tinker piper, ladies and gents. A wee something for the tinker piper!"

The tourists dropped money into her mug. One man reached out to try and pat her head – as if she was a dog, she thought indignantly, and shied away from the reaching hand. Two girls of about her own age eyed her curiously. They were wearing bright cotton tops tucked into skin-tight jeans; and with equal curiosity, she returned their stare. Those jeans, she told herself – some day, in spite of all her Nan said about such things being immodest for girls to wear, some day she would get rid of her tatty old dress and wear a pair of jeans like that, instead.

The tourists gathered around Jim when he had finished piping. The woman with the tape-recorder spoke rapidly to him, hands expressively gesturing; and when he turned away from her, there was a broad grin on his face. With a backward jerk of his head towards her, he told Ilsa and Old Nan:

"She collects folksongs, she says. Wanted me to tell her the words of the tune."

Ilsa asked, "And did you?"

"Hey, come on!" The joke had been a rich one, Jim's tone implied, but not so rich as all that! "Did you want I should have shocked the creature out of the few wits God gave her?"

Both Ilsa and Old Nan were now grinning as broadly as he was; but once the pipes were back in the cart and they were once more on their way, Cat began to hear Old Nan humming the tune her father had played. The humming changed to the sound of Old Nan singing aloud:

"O I can drink and no' get drunken,

I can fecht and no' get slain – "

The words of the following line shot through Cat's head and scandalised her with the knowledge that it was only traveller men who ever sang them – and usually drunk men, at that! From her place at the tail of the cart she called:

"Nan! Hey, Nan! You can't sing that song!"

"Away you go, lassie. When you're my age, you can do anything you damn well please!"

Old Nan's head was turned back towards Cat as she spoke. Her wrinkled face was stretched in a grin of wicked delight. Cat saw that her father and mother were also looking back towards her, and the smiles that lit their faces were confirmation of her own realisation then. Old Nan had at last come out of her mourning for Granda McPhie. Old Nan was her own tough and slyly-joking self again!

There were no tourists to bother them in the Pass of Drumochter. The Pass, with its bare, bleak hills scored by gullies still filled with long fingers of frozen snow, was no place for tourists to linger. Yet still, in spite of the cold upland wind there, the weather held; and beyond the long stretch of the Pass they came again to moorland and scattered villages. Then there were cliffs of naked red stone rising almost vertically from both sides of the road, and the road itself began to run downwards from its highest point – down, down, and down, until suddenly below them there was blue, the blue dancing waters of the Moray Firth, with the town of Inverness clustered beside it.

They skirted the town on the rising ground to its south, and descended into the traffic to cross the bridge over the

River Ness. They were heading west now, to the small glen that was Ilsa's land of heart's desire; and when they reached it on the evening of that day's journey, they made their camp by the shores of Loch Ness.

"Where Naois lived with Deirdre," Old Nan said, "when these two young people fell in love and had to flee from Ireland and the vengeance of King Conachar of Ulster, who wanted Deirdre for himself. And Naois built a tower for Deirdre here, so close to the water that he could draw a bow at the stag from the window and spear the salmon from the door."

"Is that it, the tower that Naois built?" Cat pointed to a ruined castle on the very edge of a bay where swans sailed and the rise of a fish made occasional plops in the still waters of the loch.

Old Nan laughed. "Ach, no, lassie! That castle's only five – maybe six – hundred years old. And it was a thousand years before that time that Naois and Deirdre lived out their love."

"Did they stay here till they died?" Cat stared at her grandmother, fascinated by the thought that a time so long ago could hold a tale so fresh and urgent-sounding as that of two runaway lovers.

"No," Old Nan told her. "They did not. King Conacher tricked them into going back to Ireland. And with them went the brothers of Naois, Aillean and Ardan, who had helped to guard Deirdre in her tower. But when they reached Ireland, the King treacherously killed Naois and his brothers, and laid them side by side in the one grave. And when Deirdre looked into the open grave and saw the three cold bodies lying there, her sorrow was so great that she said, *If Aillean and Ardan could hear me, they would move over and leave room for me to lie beside my love.* And the dead brothers of Naois heard her, and they moved to leave a space between them and Naois. Then Deirdre lay down in the grave, and clasped her beloved in her arms, and she died."

Cat leaned forward to a bush of the yellow-blossomed broom growing around the camp, and sniffed hard, as if to draw in its summery scent. But sniffing at the broom was only a device to ward off the tears she could have wept for the young Deirdre lying down to die beside her dead young lover.

"D'you want the rest of the story?" Old Nan asked; and in surprise and sudden hope, Cat exclaimed:

"I thought that was the end!"

"No, there's a bit more yet. The King, you see, was still jealous of Naois, even in death. And so he had Deirdre lifted and laid in another grave that was dug on the bank of a stream, opposite to the place on the stream's other bank, where the grave of Naois had been dug. Then both graves were filled in, and the King thought he had won. But a little sweet-scented pine tree grew from the grave of Naois, and another small and sweet-scented pine grew from the grave of Deirdre. The trees leant towards one another, across the stream. Their branches touched and intertwined. And so these two that King Conachar had tried to the very last to part from one another became forever united – not in the stiff clasp of death, but in the tender touch of green and growing life."

Ilsa smiled at the smile growing on Cat's features. Softly then, she said:

"Your Nan tells it like it was the story of people she knew herself. And just like it had happened yesterday – eh, Cat?"

Cat nodded, aware suddenly that her parents had

52

listened as intently as she herself had listened, and the talk turned to the practical aspects of the glen.

Jim could get at least three weeks' work there, Ilsa, said, singling turnips, hoeing, and other jobs in season. Old Nan decided that this would give her time to renew the stock of healing herbs she liked to carry with her.

"And if I make you some wooden clothes pegs," Jim told Ilsa, "that'll give you something to hawk around the doors."

But there was no need for Cat to work, of course – not when her Daddy was earning steady wages. "Though I'll come with you sometimes, Mammy," she offered, "if you need me to carry things. And the rest of the time, I think, I'll just roam around with Shuffler."

"You'd do better to spend time teaching him manners," Old Nan observed tartly, and Cat knew exactly what was meant by that. It was only two days since Shuffler had licked a plate; and the traveller rule was that any dish any animal touched could never again be considered clean. Nor had it made any difference then, that they only had one plate each. There was still no help for it but to break the one that Shuffler had licked; and Old Nan, it seemed, was still holding a grudge about that.

"You'll have to be sure to keep him close in to you too," Jim warned. "We can't afford to have farmers here blaming us for a dog running loose among sheep and cattle."

"I'll keep him well in hand," Cat promised; and so faithfully did she stick to this promise that it led her one day in her roamings to a secret she had never ever dreamed of before then.

They had been two weeks in the glen before that

happened – more than enough time for her to realise why it held such charm for her mother.

It was like being in a garden, she thought, a wilderness garden lit brightly with the yellow of gorse and broom and hawkweed, the purple of heath and heart's ease, the rose-red of fireweed. Along every track she roamed, too, was a border of tall foxglove spikes with the thimble-shaped white and pink and purple flowers her Nan called "witches' thimbles." On the lower slopes of the enclosing hills were whole meadows of sweet-scented orchids. From higher up she could see the river that tied loops of silver around the green-gold of barley fields, and the white-washed cottages of the glen looking like a scatter of white birds peacefully nestling among the green.

But those upper slopes that gave her such a vantage point were also where cattle were put to graze in summer, and on the day of her discovery a hare started up from the pasture. Shuffler took off after the hare, but she called him sharply back to her, gripped him by the scruff of the neck and ran him quickly away from the nearby cattle and into the pinewood below the pasture.

Once there, she loosed him again, and ran along one of the many deer-tracks in the forest. The path she followed sloped downwards, then levelled out for some distance before it gave on to a clearing that formed a small meadow of short, smooth grass. And there, at the centre of the grassy clearing, was her mother Ilsa. The bundles she had been carrying lay some distance from her. And she was dancing!

Ilsa was dancing with her slender body swaying light and supple as tall, wind-rippled grass, arms spread out, eyes closed, lips parted as if to drink in from the very air around her the silent music of her dance. Cat stood thunderstruck at the sight, yet still retaining enough sense to hold Shuffler, unmoving, at her side.

With a gesture smooth as water flowing, Ilsa turned in her direction. The eyes that had been closed in ecstasy, languidly opened. The opened eyes, staring at Cat, remained wide. Slowly Cat went towards her mother. Ilsa's arms dropped to her sides. Her thin face took on a guarded expression. Cat said uncertainly:

"I never knew, Mammy. I never dreamed – I mean, I've never seen you do anything like that."

"Well, it's far from the first time, if that's what you're wondering." Ilsa moved to take up her bundles, her voice sounding quite matter of fact. Cat followed, talking as she went.

"It was really great, Mammy, the way you did it. Like it was grass moving in the wind – not the way other travellers dance, shouting and jumping about, and all that. But why – I mean, dancing all alone and so different from the others – why d'you do it?"

"Because I always have. I was born that way. Like a man said to me once when I was younger even than you, I was meant to be a dancer – a real dancer, the way people do it on the stage. He wanted to train me, that man, but you can't be a real dancer and live the travelling life too. And I could never live any other kind of life. That's all there is to it. But Cat – "

Ilsa turned and found Cat staring at her in fascination. "You're not to tell anyone about this. Your Daddy knows, and I think your Nan guesses; but when I dance it's for myself alone, because it fills a need in me to dance. And sometimes too because – "

Abruptly she stopped there, biting her lip; and then, in

a voice that attempted the same matter of fact tone as before, she went on:

"You're my only living bairn, Cat. And I want more bairns. I need more bairns. But it seems I can't have them. All I have is grief for the ones I've lost – two before you came, and three afterwards. But sometimes – " The matter of fact voice roughened, and broke a little. "Sometimes, like it was with me today, I've found I can dance the grief out of me. And then, you see – " Ilsa bent to her bundles and made brisk play of swinging one on to her back. Standing straight again, she smiled at Cat. "Then I'm all right again!"

Cat looked uncertainly at her mother. In spite of all her experience to the contrary, she now had a strange and overwhelming feeling of Ilsa as some very fragile sort of creature; and with this feeling had come an odd sense of protectiveness towards her. Hesitantly she said:

"Mammy – "

"Aye, Cat?" Ilsa's face was quizzical, still faintly smiling.

"I – " Cat paused, shyness holding back the words in her mind. "I'll walk back with you," she said awkwardly, and made a quick movement to pick up the rest of Ilsa's gear.

They walked together back to the camp, with Cat still feeling that disturbing sense of protectiveness and always ready to give her mother a hand over any rough bit of ground. But Ilsa, it seemed, was quite restored to her usual rather vague and amiable self. Ilsa was striding along as lithe and graceful as always, looking the very embodiment of traveller woman hardihood; and with sidelong glances that took all this in, Cat tried hard to reconcile the Mammy she knew so well with the Mammy

56

who had been such a surprise to her.

There was to be another surprise for Cat, however, before the stay in Ilsa's little glen was over – one that was directly connected to the tragedy behind the break in her mother's voice that day. But the surprise, this time, came from her father, and it was not until their last evening in the glen that it broke on her.

It was trout they had for supper that evening, brown trout fresh from the loch and pan-fried in butter. With a long day's roaming behind her and nothing in her stomach but wild berries, Cat ate voraciously; but as soon as her hunger was satisfied, she began asking the questions roused by her ever-lively curiosity about her father's poaching methods.

"How'd you catch this lot, Daddy?"

"Otter board." Jim threw back a piece of sacking that had concealed something lying beside him on the grass. The something was an inch-thick piece of wood, oval-shaped, inset with a keel, and with long streamers of nylon thread attached to it. At intervals along the threads were the artificial flies he used as trout-lures. Coiled beside the board and fixed to one end of it was a long piece of twine.

"And when you're using it," he informed her, "it looks kind of like the head of an otter just breaking the surface of the water – which, of course, is why they call it an otter board."

"What makes it ride out from the bank?" Cat stroked the little keel with an exploring finger. "This keel?"

"Aye – provided you can first set the thing at the proper angle in the water."

"And when it's far enough from the bank you pull it along with this twine – is that right?"

"Aye, right again. The streamers with the flies float out from it then, the board rides along parallel to the bank, and if there's trout in the water at all, you'll have them for supper."

Cat studied the otter-board again, wondering just how to judge that "proper angle" for setting it in the water. For a moment or so she puzzled over this, and then spoke as unthinkingly as she had on the day she had wanted to go with Charlie Drummond on his pearling expedition.

"Would you show me how to set the board, Daddy?"

"Why not? I'll do better than that, in fact, because – " Her father hesitated long enough to exchange looks with her mother, and then finished, "because I'd like to teach you all my skills, Cat."

"But you can't!" In shocked amazement, Cat snatched her hand away from the otter board. "You'd make a split mechanic of me!"

Split mechanic! Jim McPhie winced instinctively to hear his daughter voicing a term so abusive of her own sex.

"Aye," he admitted. "That's what they'd call you." Once again, there was that look between him and her mother; and, as if taking heart from it, he added, "Those that are foul-mouthed, at least. But the way things are with your Mammy, would you really blame me for that?"

"Cat – " Her mother spoke quietly. "I've told him about the way I spoke to you that day in the woods, or he would never have mentioned this idea to you. So just think, hen. He's got no son to follow him, no laddie he can teach his skills to. What's more, he never will have a son. And that's a terrible thing for a traveller man to face – to know that all his skills will die with him."

"Unless you learn them." Old Nan's voice coming in at

the end of Ilsa's argument brought Cat facing around in outrage and still greater astonishment at finding even her grandmother approving the thought of herself as that terrible thing, a split mechanic.

"And what if I do? I'll never get married then, will I? Not to any traveller man, at least."

"Who told you that?"

"Charlie Drummond – one day when I wanted to go with him to fish mussels for pearls."

"Ach!" Old Nan took her pipe from her mouth and spat contemptuously into the fire. "What does a laddie like him know! Just that traveller men are old-fashioned about some things, that's all. But I tell you, Cat, any one of them that wants to marry you some day will do just that – if the love he feels for you is true love, that is."

"Like your Daddy still feels for me," Ilsa's quiet voice added; "even though I never have managed to bear him the son he craves to have."

Cat looked from her mother to her grandmother. Old Nan was smoking again, her face impassive. Ilsa's face wore the strained look it had carried when she spoke about the dead babies. Cat felt her outrage melting, her astonishment fading into the kind of understanding they both seemed to feel for her father. As for Charlie Drummond and the way he had spoken that day – well, they knew a lot more about such things than Charlie, didn't they?

"You'd be quick to learn too." The eager sound of her father's voice interrupted her train of thought. "You ask the right kind of questions. And you're interested. Anybody can see that."

"I know I am, Daddy. I know." Cat paused, wrestling now with the positive temptation her father's offer had begun to hold for her. "And I really would like to be able to do the kind of things you can teach me. But my friends – they'd tease me if I did. I'd come in for an awful lot of teasing."

"No, you wouldn't. Not from the laddies, anyway, because I'd train that big Shuffler brute along with you, you see. And any laddie would be jealous of your being the boss of such a fine working dog as he'd make. So it's you, Cat, that would have the last laugh at them."

Cat leaned forward to hug her knees in sudden pleasure at the thought of at last being able to lord it over big fellows like Alec and Charlie. And Shuffler, she thought, Shuffler who'd been so awkward as a pup that he'd been spared the fate of drowning only when she had begged to have him for her own, Shuffler who had repaid her with such constant devotion that he was like a second shadow to her – what a swagger he'd be able to cut then! Except with Rhona, of course. Rhona had always thought she was daft to make so much of Shuffler; and so what would Rhona say to her being a split mechanic? With her pleasure banished by the thought of the scorn she would have to face from Rhona, she objected:

"But it would be different with Rhona. Because she's a girl, you see."

Old Nan said suddenly, "There's something you'd better learn sooner than later, Cat. If Rhona truly is your friend, she'll stay your friend. But if her friendship's the kind that can't stand you being a bit out of the ordinary compared to herself, then it's the kind that isn't worth a hoot in hell to anybody."

And *that* made sense, Cat told herself. Her glance slid way from Old Nan to linger again on the otter board, and she was aware of her insides beginning to churn with the kind of excitement she always felt in moments of anticipation. She looked up to find the eyes of the other three intently fixed on her.

"But remember, Cat," her father said, "nobody's trying to force you into this. The choice is yours; and whatever one you make, none of us will blame you for it."

"That's true," Ilsa confirmed. "Man, woman, or child, everyone has the right to make of their life what they want to make of it."

"Because every single life has its own importance," Old Nan chimed in: "which is why a body should always be free to live as that one wants to live. That's what travellers believe, anyway, Cat. And if you're still wondering what makes us different from other people, *that's* where the difference lies."

As if by common consent then, the three of them began to rise so that she could be left alone to decide. But the temptation of the otter board had now become altogether too much for Cat, and her choice was already made. She scrambled to her feet, the otter board in her hand.

"Come on, Daddy!" She faced her father, the excitement in her rising to its peak and putting a breathless gasp into her voice. "There's time yet tonight to let you show me how to use this!"

6

With her back pressed into a hollow of the hillside, the grass cold beneath her but Shuffler's body hugged warmly to her side, Cat patiently waited out the time of half-light before the dawn. It was in this half-light that the rabbits on the hill would venture out to feed. That was one of the many lessons she had learned since the night her father had taught her how to use the otter board, and she could set rabbit snares now with the best of them. But Shuffler had been learning too, as they travelled still farther north, and now it was his turn to show how well he remembered his lessons.

A flush of pinkish light appeared on the eastern horizon. Shuffler stirred. He raised his head, nostrils questing the air.

"Quiet," Cat whispered, and clamped both hands firmly around his jaws. Not that Shuffler was naturally a noisy dog, of course, but he was still young enough to be excited into barking when he scented the rabbits; and a dog that could not be trusted to keep both still and silent even when it was within pouncing distance of game of any kind, would be no use at all to Cat McPhie, poacher.

"And so there must always be an action to go with each word of command," her father had instructed her. "A hand laid flat on his back for 'Down', a grip that makes it impossible for him to bark, for 'Quiet' – that sort of thing. Then, you'll find, he'll begin to connect the word with what's done when you say it; and in time, the action itself will be enough to command him."

A rabbit lolloped into view. Shuffler's whole body quivered at the sight of it. His head jerked convulsively, but Cat kept her hands clamped tight around his jaws and whispered again:

"Quiet. Quiet. Quiet."

The eastern light strengthened, became tinged with gold. A lark sprang from the grass and spiralled upwards, sending a long trill of song back to earth as it rose. In the growing light, Cat could see that the hillside was alive with the grey, feeding forms of rabbits. Her father came creeping towards her, the lean brown form of Sheba slinking at his heels. He nodded towards Shuffler and whispered:

"Try him out."

Cat removed her hands, and Shuffler did not bark. He did not move either, but watched her intently instead until she gave the forward hand-wave that meant "Seek!" Instantly then, he shot away from her like a black charge out of some enormous cannon. Her father grinned at the sight and said:

"Seek, Sheba."

Sheba followed Shuffler's charge at the pace suited to her mature years. Sheba knew, in any case, what Shuffler was only beginning to learn – that rabbits are predictable creatures. The ones scattering now to the hoped-for safety of their burrows would take the paths they always used; and – especially at this season of the year when they were young and inexperienced – it would take no great effort to make a kill among them.

"It's hare we'll have to train Shuffler to next," Jim remarked. "But before we do that, Cat, tell me why you think that a hare that's being chased by a dog will always choose to run uphill."

Cat pondered the question, and said finally, "Because of its shape – is that it? Short front legs, big, powerful back legs – a hare must always be faster at running uphill than running down."

"Right! And a hare will always take the same escape route out of a field. And so, when you go after hare with Shuffler, be sure you choose a field that has a slope to it with the gate at the upper end of the slope. You set Sheba on guard to block the hare's bolt-hole. Then slip Shuffler into the field, net the gate, and he'll drive the hare straight into the net for you."

Together they cleaned the rabbits that the dogs brought proudly back to them. The crows and buzzards that had been gathering as they talked, swooped down on the leavings, and they made their way back to the camp along the track of a stream where, Jim said, they should be able to have a look at some otters.

The otters were at the place where he had found signs of them, a whole family all merrily playing at sliding on their backsides down the smooth, grassy bank of the stream, to land with a plop in the water and an eel-like turn that brought them gliding in to the bank to start all over again.

"They're playing at keeping the pot boiling," Cat whispered to her father; and smilingly, he nodded agreement. They edged away from their watching-point, and once they were well clear of it, he told her:

"And you've a lot more of such sights to see yet, I promise you – because the beauty of this sort of work is that you just can't practise it till you first know the ways of wild creatures. And in the end, you know, you get to love those creatures so much that you do more watching of them than hunting."

"But what about when it comes to killing them?" Cat looked doubtfully down at the rabbits dangling cross-legged from the length of fence-wire in her hand. "That's not so good, is it?"

"Of course it's not. But how d'you think any creature in the wild dies? There's one of only four causes, Cat – starvation, disease, accident, or falling prey to some other creature. Now which of those deaths would you choose – and think carefully before you speak because the first two are slow and painful, the third can be the same as the first two; but creatures that kill to live – the owl, the eagle, the fox, and so on, always kill quickly. And it's the same with you and me *and* the dogs – isn't it?"

"All right," Cat told him. "You win there. But I still don't like the killing part."

"Nobody does – except those fellows that call them-selves 'sportsmen'. They're the only creatures on earth that kill for pleasure. But folks like us, Cat, we kill for the pot; or maybe sometimes to sell so that we'll have something to put in the pot. Which reminds me. . . " Her father pointed downhill to where the stream of the otters became a waterfall dropping into a ravine. "Down in that ravine there, is a fine salmon water. And once we get even farther north, I've been thinking, I'll have to show you how you can take a salmon."

"But Daddy – " Cat's reaction to this was one of such alarm that it brought her to a sudden halt. "Taking wild rabbits off the hill, Daddy, that's one thing. But poaching a salmon river – you know fine it's dead against the law to do that!"

"So was using the otter board." Her father, too, had halted, and was looking at her in amused surprise. "But I didn't hear you making a great song about the law when you tried it."

"I wasn't thinking that night," Cat defended herself. "Not about the law, anyway. And you know fine too that it isn't nearly so bad to take a few trout as it is to poach salmon. I've heard you say it yourself. The Sheriff wouldn't be hard on you over the trout. But salmon – that's game for gentry. That's why they have all those keepers and bailiffs on the prowl for folk like us. And so we'd both be for the high jump, wouldn't we, if we went after salmon?"

"If we're caught," Jim agreed. "But I've been too long at this game to let that happen. And besides, you that's so bothered about the laws against poaching – just look there!" With one pointing hand he drew Cat's attention to the panorama of moor and hill, loch and river and field, sweeping away on all sides of them.

"All that, as far as we can see, belongs to one man. Or, at least, the law says it does. But was that what God intended when he made this earth – that one man should be able to say, 'This is *my* mountain, *my* loch, *my* river'?"

Cat shook her head in wondering denial of such an idea. Besides which, she told herself, to own a *mountain* – that was just ridiculous! How could any man say he owned a mountain, any more than he could say he owned the sea, or the sky?

"Right, then," her father continued. Was it not God also that put the trout and salmon in the water, the same as it was Him that put the hares in the field, the rabbits on the hill? And so, when I take any of these creatures for the pot, am I not just taking of the bounty he put there for all of us other creatures?"

"I suppose you are," Cat admitted; and walked onwards thinking how strange it was that God should have one purpose and men should make laws to twist it to something quite other than He had intended. A memory of the sergeant who had accused her of stealing pheasant eggs flashed into her mind and made her smile inwardly at the thought of what *that* big polis would have to say to her father's argument.

Her amusement deepened into a feeling of reckless delight in the new dimension her life had assumed; and the feeling was so strong that she knew instinctively she could never go back on it, never be other than she was then – a traveller, one who had been born to woman's work, but still one who had crossed the barrier that would have stopped her finally having *all* the traveller skills at her command.

"I'm Cat," the feeling whispered; "Cat, herself. Never mind the polis or the settled folk. Never mind what Rhona says, or Alec, or Charlie. I'll go my own way. And there's nothing, nobody, will ever stop me."

"Have patience," her father counselled when she reminded him about showing her how to take salmon. "There's a few things have to come together before the occasion's right for that."

Carefully, then, he explained what he had in mind. They would make it a daylight job – water bailiffs being in the habit of patrolling their beats principally in the night hours when salmon poachers were most likely to be abroad. But operating in daylight also meant they would have to be very quick about it, and so they would have to choose a time when they were on a stretch of road running close to the river. And further to avoid being seen, that stretch would have to be distant from human habitation. As for the gaff they would use, there was no traveller could risk being caught with such a thing in his possession, and so –

"Look here!" Jim reached into one pocket that produced a strong steel hook, into another that yielded a length of thin twine. "Here's the makings of one – see! You bind the hook on to a length of stout hazelwood with the twine – 'whipping', they call that, and you choose hazel because it grows so straight. You do that job on the spot – quickly. And before you leave, you undo it again just as quickly. So you'd better get some practice in at it, eh?"

Cat looked up from the hook as he spoke, and saw that he was grinning over the words, his dark face alight with a feeling she could sense as being akin to her own at the moment she had vowed always to be "Cat herself." A repeat of that emotion shot through her, and with her own grin flashing out in response to his, she told him:

"Don't worry. I will!"

"Good. But for safety's sake on your first try, you'd still better leave it to me to make the gaff. But even so, there's a lot more yet for you to learn. And so – "

More soberly now, her father began to instruct her on the business of actually using the gaff. From there, he went on to give her instructions for the precision timing that would be needed for the venture; and when the day for it finally came, she was alert to do instantly as he did.

The bank leading down to the chosen part of the river was a steep, grassy slope. The pool at the foot of the slope was screened by trees. As Pibroch drew the cart level with the trees, Cat and her father swerved aside from the road. The cart trundled slowly onwards while they went at a sliding run down the bank. They gained the shelter of the trees and knelt, side by side, at the edge of the pool.

"There!" Jim pointed downwards. The pool was one well known to him from previous journeys, so that he knew exactly how and where to look for salmon resting on their way upriver to spawn in shallower water. "Shade your eyes from the light striking the water," he told Cat, "and then you'll see it."

Quickly then, he rose and began whipping the hook on to the end of his stick of hazelwood. Cat put a hand to her brow and bent closer to the water. A pale something faintly glimpsed in its amber colour developed outline and took on a more positive gleam.

"See it?" She looked up at the sound of her father's voice and realised that, for all the speed of his movements, he was making a very secure job of binding the hook on to the stick.

"I think so." Peering again into the water, she became aware that she could now see the dark line of the fish's back above the paleness of its flank, a light flicker that was the movement of a ventral fin. She felt her father's body pressed against her own as he returned to his kneeling position beside her, and without taking her eyes from the water, she reached a hand for the gaff.

"I see it properly now, facing upstream from me."

The gaff was slid into her hand. She could see the whole of the salmon now, lying perfectly still, although the refraction of light on the water made its shape waver. Gently she began to lower the hooked end of the gaff into the water behind its curving tail.

"Slow, Cat, slow," her father breathed. "Slide the hook forward slow. Keep it well under the fish's body. And when you strike with it, strike *hard!* I'll help you take the weight of it coming up."

She was now fully down on one knee, her right knee, her body bent flat forward over the knee, her left leg stretched out behind her. The strike that would drive the hook into the fish, and the heave that brought it out of the water, would have to be performed all in the one motion. And to enable her to give that upward heave, she would have to throw her body back, and sideways. But the position she was in now, she reckoned, would allow her to do so.

The fish had not moved. Downstream from it, as she was, she was out of the range of its vision. The hook was sliding farther and farther along underneath it. Her grip on the handle of the gaff was still rock-steady. *Now!* She jerked the hook hard into the strike, heaving upwards on the gaff, throwing her body back and sweeping her arm sideways up from the water. The wrenching pain that shot through her shoulder muscles forced a cry from her; but even as her mouth opened on the sound, her father's hand clamped over her own hold on the gaff, the force of his strength was added to her own effort, and the salmon shot in a gleaming arc from water to land.

"Stand shot, now!" Her father's command brought her to her feet and sent her running to keep the lookout from the edge of the sheltering clump of trees. He lifted a stone as she rose, and gave the one blow to the head that killed the salmon. There was no sign of anyone on the slope of green between them and the road, or on the road itself, and minutes later they had overtaken the cart still trundling slowly along, the hook and twine safely back in Jim's pocket, the salmon hidden with its head end under his shirt, the tail end slid down inside one trouser leg.

It was a hen fish, a twelve-pounder, and clean-run. Old

Nan cackled with glee as Jim stowed it in the cart, in the shelter of her spreading skirts. Ilsa smiled her slow smile at the look of tingling pride on Cat's face. But the operation, they all knew, was still far from finished. True, they had taken every precaution against being caught in the act. But a traveller family with something to hide could not afford to attract the slightest notice, and it would take only one suspiciously-minded person to phone the water bailiff with a warning that would certainly bring him hot-foot to demand a search of their cart.

Quickly Jim guided Pibroch on to a westward-leading side track that would take them well away from the river before it circled to rejoin the northbound road. The detour he had in mind, also, took in a village that boasted one of the few tourist hotels in the area; and late that evening, after they had made a well-concealed camp outside the village, Jim took the salmon to the back door of the hotel's kitchen.

Cat went with him, out of curiosity to discover how the selling of the salmon would be done; and learned, to her surprise, that no words were needed. A woman in cook's dress answered her father's gentle knock at the kitchen door. There was a brief gleam in the dusk as he unwrapped a corner of the sacking that hid the salmon. The woman retreated indoors, and came back a few seconds later. The salmon changed hands. Her father pocketed the money the cook held furtively out to him. But how much money? Cat wondered as they walked back to the camp, and ventured finally to ask the question aloud.

"Just what the wifie chose to give." Her father shrugged, and sighed a little with his answer. "And that wasn't much. But what d'you expect, lassie? A cheap price is all you'll ever get for a salmon with no questions asked about where it came from. Though they'll charge dear enough for it, the folk that run these hotels, when they serve it up to their posh customers!"

Cat walked on thinking of hotel-keepers making a fat profit and rich customers stuffing their bellies. All at her expense, too! But did that matter, really, so long as they made enough out of it to live on for a few days? And for her too, of course, there was still the memory of the excitement in that dash towards the river, the thrill of spotting the salmon, the glory of the moment that had sent the fish arcing over her head. And besides – Her mind blundered suddenly on another aspect of the situation.

Salmon were creatures of the wild – part of God's creation. And so it wasn't at *her* expense that the hoteliers and their customers were enjoying themselves, because the salmon she had gaffed had not belonged to her any more than it had belonged to the man who claimed to own the river. She laughed aloud at this last thought, and her father looked down at her to ask:

"What's tickling you, then?"

Cat told him what she had been thinking. Her father chuckled and said:

"Aye. The joke's on him, all right. And besides, lassie, for all *we* know that same bloke might well have his dinner at that hotel tomorrow night – and be one o' those that have to pay dear to eat that salmon!"

The two of them were still laughing at this by the time they reached camp; and when Ilsa asked the reason for their laughter, Jim told her:

"Nothing much, lass. Just the same sort of thing that Himself up there must laugh at sometimes. And young Cat McPhie, it seems, likes the same kind of joke."

7

The road north became a narrow one, a single-track highway that saw very little traffic. The villages were now few and far between. There was little cultivation, and so the occasions when Jim could earn something from farm work also became fewer. Not that there was any danger of them starving, of course, when they could get rabbits and trout and other game; but they still had to find basics like flour and oatmeal, and Ilsa had nothing left to trade for these.

"But we'll soon mend that," Jim said cheerfully, and began to show Cat how to make what he called "heather besoms" – brooms made from bunches of bellheather roots trimmed to a uniform length and then wired to long handles of hazelwood. As he pointed out to her, too, they were just right for using as stable-brooms, these heather besoms, and so Ilsa had no difficulty in trading them at the isolated farms on their way.

The women on these farms, also, lived such lonely lives that they were glad of a chance to talk to Ilsa, sometimes even to invite her into the kitchen for a cup of tea; and if it came out in the gossip over the tea that Ilsa had 'the gift', the woman would beg to have her fortune told.

Ilsa would take the woman's teacup then, turning it in her hand and telling her things from the pattern of the tealeaves left clinging inside it after the tea had been drunk. "Reading the cup", it was called, and Ilsa was good at that because it wasn't only the shape of the leaves that told her the things she saw. Much more than that, it was the fact of holding in her hand something that the other woman had held – that was what really allowed the gift to come through in her.

The woman would always be pleased by her fortune, too, because Ilsa was always careful to mention only the good things in it; and then there would be something extra added to the flour, or butter, or milk already exchanged for the besom – a packet of tea perhaps, or even a twist of the husband's tobacco to be carried proudly back to Jim and Old Nan.

So they continued to survive as they had always done, living from hand to mouth while the road wound onwards, ribboning its grey length around hill and over river, rising and falling and rising again, with the summit of each new rise seeming like yet another small horizon pulling them farther on and farther on. And in camp each evening, Cat watched the blue pipe smoke curling up to mingle with the grey smoke of the fire. She listened to all the talk that went on in quiet, murmuring voices that filled her mind with the wonder of one story after another. She caressed the sleeping head that Shuffler had laid on her knee, and was utterly content – except for one thing.

She had a secret of her own now, one that sometimes gave her pangs of conscience. And it was Shuffler who was the cause of it.

Shuffler loved to swim. It was the strain of labrador in him which accounted for that. And July in the Highlands meant rain that had swelled all the lochs and rivers on their way. Very often, then, when she had finished helping her father to renew the stock of heather besoms and her mother was away hawking at some distant farm, she had taken Shuffler off to have his swim.

No harm in that, certainly; but it was when she saw how much he was enjoying himself that she took to plunging in after him. And that was where the guilt feelings came in.

Not that there was any harm, either, of course, in taking a plunge into river water. She had been forced into it often enough before when there was no other way of getting clean. But that had always been with her mother standing by to guard against intruders on her nakedness; and a lot of fuss, too, about washing her hair, and protests about soap stinging her eyes. But this was different, this secret cavorting with Shuffler. This was for fun, only. And how she loved it!

She yelled each time she hit the water and felt the shock of its cold against her skin, yelled with the same kind of exhilaration that had gripped her on the day she had run barefoot in the cuckoo snow. Then, as her body adjusted to the temperature of the water, came a different delight in the sensuous feeling of its smoothness rippling over her – and with no fear of its depth either, even although she could not swim. Shuffler always kept close to her, so that all she had to do when she got out of her depth was to grasp the thick ruff of hair at his neck and float beside him as he swam into shallower water.

She could depend on Shuffler too, to bark a warning of anyone approaching her swimming-place; but occasionally also, she was prompted by those guilt feelings to add her own watchfulness to his. Her father, after all, was so very strict over her being modest about her body – every bit as strict as other traveller daddies were with their daughters. And so what would *he* say to this chance she was taking – swimming naked where strangers might see her?

What would any traveller man say?

A strange feeling came over her on the day this second question shot through her mind – the same eerie kind of feeling she had experienced months before when it seemed she had heard a voice that was her own voice yet still one that was strangely unlike hers loudly saying, *I'll never travel with your family, Charlie.*

But this time it was Charlie's voice she could hear, Charlie angrily telling her, *You've shamed me, Cat McPhie. You've put terrible shame on me.* This time also, it seemed to her, the Cat McPhie he said that to was a figure older than she was then, a figure crouched down at the foot of a tree, hysterically weeping and shivering. And this Cat McPhie, too, was naked.

August, after the July rains, was bright and clear. August was the month when Cat spent nights learning to "burn the water" for sea-trout, first checking that the water bailiff was well away from the chosen part of the river, then wading upstream with the flashlight in her left hand held close to the water, the gaff in her right hand poised to strike at the fish held immobile by the flashlight's powerful beam. And August was also the month which brought them on to a scene that held her speechless with wonder.

Here, she saw, there were no green hills close at hand, no twisting and hummocked road beckoning with small horizons. On all sides here, there was moor with a road that arrowed straight across it and ran on, seemingly, to infinity. The moor itself blazed purple with a solid growth of flowering heather touched with fugitive gleams of light from scattered lochs and rivers. The seeming bounds of the moor were mountains, jagged, and coloured hazy-blue with distance.

But the sky above the moor and its ring of mountains was so high, so huge, so piled with great cloud masses alternating with such vast expanses of blue, that even beyond the mountains there was an impression of light and distance. And so here, it seemed to her wondering gaze, there was no horizon. Here, with that enormous sky arching above her, she had the feeling that she was walking on the very roof of the world!

A question shot through her mind. Was this it – Old Nan's enchanted land; this blue and purple and silver land of light and endless distance? Had they reached it at last? She ran forward to the front of the cart to ask her question, and was impatient when Old Nan answered:

"Not yet, Cat. Not yet. Though we're on the edge of it now, at least. And soon, very soon, you'll see the full glory of it."

"It's morning now," she persisted. "How soon is 'very soon'?"

Old Nan pointed ahead to a mountain that had a peculiarly uneven shape. "That's Ben Loyal," she instructed. "Keep your eyes on that. Once we've crossed the moor and got to the other side of Ben Loyal, we'll be there."

Cat kept her eyes on Ben Loyal as far as her engrossment with the thought of walking on the roof of the world would allow her to do; and by the late afternoon of that day they had crossed the moor. Close at hand on their right, then, was a big loch, and equally close on their left was the mountain.

"Loch Loyal," Old Nan named the loch for them, but

Cat had eyes only for the mountain of that name. Rugged and high it loomed over them, its tumble of grey rock walls looking like a pile of castles built by giants, only to be cast into ruins by a race of even bigger giants. The straight road twisted to wind around it. The great castles fell away to green slopes. The road turned again, till once more they had grey rock soaring up on their left, this time with a sheen of water ahead of them.

"Sea water," Old Nan said and a few minutes later they saw that the water was indeed a sea inlet, wide at its mouth, tapering to a point at its inland end. "The Kyle of Tongue," Old Nan named the inlet for them. "And this is where we'll camp tonight."

The smile wrinkles at the corners of her eyes deepened as she spoke; and even if the prospect before them had not already told them that they had arrived at her enchanted land, the look of perfect content on her face would have been enough to say that this was so. They stood staring, all of them, at the view that opened out all around from the crest of the slope that led down to the Kyle.

On their left soared the crags of Ben Loyal, with the sun's evening rays making a separately gold-outlined castle of each of its peaks. In the distance ahead and on their right were other mountains, misty-blue, with the hollows between them seeming like bowls brimming with the same evening gold. At the foot of the slope, the waters of the Kyle lay in swathes of colour that ranged from the dark blue of its far waters, through ultramarine and cornflower blue, to the pale greeny-blue turquoise of the shallowest water inshore.

There were seagulls wheeling and drifting above the Kyle, terns that dived on closed wings like white arrows shooting into the water. Tucked away at the foot of the slope was a small village with cottages built of stone as grey as the mountain soaring above it. And overall there was still that enormous sky that created light upon light, and distance upon endless distance.

"And it'll be places like this from now on." Old Nan's voice broke the silence of wonder that held them all. "Everywhere along this northern seacoast you'll find such places, every one of them the work of God's hands when He was young and putting His best into the making of the world."

They all smiled at this. "But that," said Jim, and pointed to the stone causeway running across the Kyle, "that's the work o' man's hand. And it looks gey new to me."

"Oh, aye, that's new," Old Nan agreed. "Finished two to three years ago, in 1971, they say. And what would Donald McKay have given for the engineers that built it, instead of having to put up with the terrible box of work-fairies that was all he had to build his causeway!"

"Who was Donald McKay?" Cat asked; but her question had to keep while they made camp for that night.

Jim pitched the tent in a sheltered hollow at the top of the slope. Ilsa gathered sticks for the fire while Old Nan got out a pan and the last of their oatmeal. They could have gone down into the village to buy some food for their supper, of course – if they'd had any money, that is, or anything left to trade, and if any of them had wanted to go down into the village. But somehow, it seemed, to stay there at their vantage point, with some fried oatmeal for their supper, was all that any of them wanted, anyway.

Cat's share of the work was to unyoke Pibroch; and, as usual, she let him search the pocket of her dress for his sweet bite. He found the sugar lumps she had been saving for him, then nudged her for more; and again as usual, she wished she had more to give him. Pibroch was old now. Gently she stroked his soft nose and wondered how much longer they would have him.

"Your supper, girl," Old Nan called. She joined the others at the fire; and when they had finished eating, went with them to sit once more and look out in silence over the Kyle.

The sun was off its waters now, and with the draining away of the gold had come an effect of light that made the Kyle look as if a veil of silver gossamer had been drawn over it. Ben Loyal, above the delicate trail of silver, had become a black, crenellated fortress. The distant mountains had lost their outlines and gone too were their brimming hollows, but the vanished sun was still sending up rays of light that turned the clouds above the mountains into floating islands of gold, the islands, too, drained of their gold. The sky in which they had floated became banded with pale green, and rosy pink, and turquoise. Cat spoke, her eyes fixed in fascination on the sky's changing colours, but her curiosity about the interrupted story still very much alive in her.

"Who *was* Donald McKay, Nan?"

"Well, it was like this," Old Nan began, and drew Cat into the crook of her arm. "In a time long gone, a man called Donald McKay that was lord of all the country hereabouts had a sweetheart living on the far side of the Kyle from him, and it was a terrible bother to him to be always watching the tides when he took a boat to row out to her. But it was either that or riding for miles on the road that runs round the head of the Kyle; and so he got more and more annoyed over his problem, until one day he met the Devil and had a wrestling match with him.

"Now Donald was a big strong man, and what with that and the bad temper that was on him, he won the match. And for a reward, the Devil gave him a box of work fairies. Or, at least, he thought it was a reward, because the first thing he set those creatures to do was to build a causeway across the Kyle so that he could walk over to see his sweetheart; and they did that job so quick it fairly took his breath away. But was that the end of it? Not at all, for these work fairies always had to be up and doing.

"Give us work!" they screamed. "Give us work!" and pestered poor Donald until he was near out of his wits trying to find them work to do – because every job he gave them you see, they finished in no time at all. But at last he hit on a way to keep the creatures occupied.

"Go you," he commanded, "and make me a rope of sand that will stretch from one side of the Kyle to the other." So off they rushed to make the rope of sand, but no sooner had they got the rope finished than the tide came up and swept it away, and they had to start all over again. It was the same the next time, and the next, and the next, just like it always will be the same. And so, I do believe, making a rope of sand is what they are still doing to this very day."

There was silence again at the end of the story; and it was Old Nan who broke the silence, speaking softly, as if to herself:

"But I'll not tell that story again. Not ever. It belongs here, you see, and this is the last time I'll see my enchanted land."

81

Nobody spoke. Nobody contradicted her. What was the use when she had simply taken her own way of stating the truth that an old woman like her was near the end of all her travelling? Jim turned his face from the others so that they would not see the tears brimming from his eyes. Ilsa put out a hand to comfort him. Cat moved closer against Old Nan. The arm that held her tightened. Her mind drifted, and was suddenly at some point in time when she felt it was some other arm that held her; and dreamily out of this feeling, she said:

"But I'll come back here, Nan. I'll come back with Charlie."

"Charlie?"

"Charlie Drummond. I'll come back with him, and it'll be his arm round me then."

"Why d'you say that, lassie? What makes you speak that way?"

"I don't know, Nan." With sleep beginning to creep up on her, Cat yawned. "All I do know is what I've just told you." Yawning again, she gave up the effort to keep her eyes open. Her head drooped against Old Nan. The old woman looked towards Ilsa. Ilsa's face was turned towards her and Cat. Ilsa had been listening. Old Nan spoke softly to her.

"Cat's reached the age when the gift begins to break through. And it's showing in her now. This bairn of yours, Ilsa, has the gift."

"I know." Ilsa spoke as softly as Old Nan had spoken. "I've been watching her, these months past, and I know."

Cat heard their voices, but only as a dim, mysterious murmur that seemed to reach her out of some far distance. Old Nan nodded towards Jim. He rose, gathered Cat in his arms, and carried her towards the tent.

Gently he laid her down inside it; and by the time he backed away from her she was deep into her first night's sleep in the enchanted land.

Interlude

"That's them!" Sergeant McKendrick gestured from the open window on his side of the patrol car; and with his gaze following the direction pointed by the finger levelled at the traveller encampment in the field beside the farmhouse, Constable Miller asked doubtfully:

"But how can you be sure it's the same lot?"

"I'll tell you how I can be sure." The sergeant turned a reproving glare on his subordinate. "I do my homework, Miller – enough to let me know that the tinks we turned out of Wilson's Wood in the time of the late snow in April this year are the same ones that come south to these parts every year in October to work for Jack Brownlee, once they've finished with the tattie harvest in Perthshire. So it's got to be them. See?"

Constable Miller dutifully saw, and both men got out of the car to look for the farmer, Jack Brownlee.

He was in the stables of his farm, admiring a couple of ponies that showed good lines under their ungroomed appearance; and he was quite willing to tell the sergeant that, yes, the travellers encamped in his field were McPhies, MacDonalds, and Drummonds. It was from Big Andy McPhie, in fact, that he had bought the two ponies.

"For my two wee granddaughters," he confided, smiling, benignly nodding his white head and then bending his tall, thin form to run an expert hand over the withers of the pony nearest to him. "Good stock, you see.

They'll make grand mounts for the lasses at the Pony Club."

"Aye, maybe." Sergeant McKendrick was not interested in grandchildren or in pony clubs. "But this lot of tinks, they're the ones that used to camp in Wilson's Wood before it was chopped down this summer to make way for the housing estate that's there now – "

"And a pity that was too," Brownlee interrupted, "to destroy such a bonny place!"

"Ach, away!" A wood, so far as Sergeant McKendrick was concerned, was a disorderly part of the landscape, and his tone made plain his view on that score. "Better far some nice, neat rows of houses than that rubbish. Anyway, what I'm telling you is this. They're thieves, that crowd, just like the rest of these damn travellers – "

"Away, man!" Now it was the old farmer's turn to be contemptuous, but indulgently so, as if dismissing some nonsensical remark from a child. "You'll get thieves among travellers, I agree, same as you'll get thieves anywhere. But you can't blame all of them for the few bad ones, can you? Besides, I know this lot. They've been coming here every year of their lives to pick tatties. Aye, and in my daddy's time it was their daddies and mammies that came. The Mist People we used to call them then."

"Mist People?" Constable Miller joined suddenly in the conversation, his rather wooden face lighting with curiosity. "How'd you come by that name?"

"Now look here – " Sergeant McKendrick held up a large authoritative hand to check the farmer's answer; but Brownlee waved him away with all of an old man's determination to speak of a beloved and vanished past.

"Let me just tell the laddie," he protested. "No harm in telling." Confidingly then, he took Constable Miller by the elbow and led him from the stable, out to where they could see the whole panorama of field and woodland beyond the field that held the traveller camp.

"See there?" he asked. "Well then, the travellers that passed through these parts when I was a laddie used to go on foot – whole families of them with the bairns trudging behind their mammies and daddies, and all of them loaded with gear. Or sometimes, maybe, they'd have a wee cart for the gear, with a pony in the shafts and the smallest of the bairns getting a ride on the cart. But you had to have sharp eyes to spot their camps, I can tell you; because it was always as quiet and sudden as the mist they came, and they vanished again the same way."

The old man was smiling now. He dropped his hold on Constable Miller's arm, and leaned on the fence rail beside them, his eyes taking on a look of remembering, the smile sounding in his voice as he spoke again.

"I mind, aye I mind when I was a bairn the surprise it always was to see their wee, round tents and their ponies in a field that was just empty space before then. Or maybe you'd come across the tents pitched in some secret corner of a wood that nobody except a wee laddie like yourself would wander into. Then the next time you looked for the tents and the ponies, they were all gone – just like mist that had melted away."

The sergeant made a loud, throat-clearing sound, and advanced to the fence. The old man straightened, looked at the constable, and told him:

"So that's how they came by that name – 'The Mist People.' D'you see now?"

The sergeant repeated his throat-clearing sound and said sternly, "Aye, well, Mr Brownlee. But it's all beat-up old cars and trailers with tinks nowadays. And you can't be secret with that sort of thing, can you? Eyesores – that's what tink camps are, these days. And it's disgusting, too, the way they're getting closer and closer to the towns, till some of them are pitched right on decent folks' doorsteps."

Mr Brownlee sighed. "It's a problem, I agree. But it's not of their making, is it? Look at the way the tourist trade's boomed these past years, with luxury hotels and holiday villages springing up all over what used to be empty countryside. And the amount of roadbuilding that's gone on, with even more countryside swallowed up by these fancy new four-lane highways. Just think of the number of traditional traveller sites that've been lost because of all that, and ask yourself – if these poor folks can't make use of any bit of waste ground they can find, what else are they to do?"

"I have asked myself." Sergeant McKendrick's voice was no less stern than before. "And you'll get my answer in due course. But first of all, let's consider this. These tinks are here with your permission, and I've no control over that. Also, you need their labour for the tattie harvest – "

"And they need the money they can earn from it!" Swiftly Mr Brownlee interrupted. "They need that cash to help see them through the winter."

"True," the sergeant agreed. "Nobody can call me an unreasonable man, and I admit the truth of that. But it still doesn't alter the fact that your farm is on *my* patch, so far as upholding the law is concerned. So tell me now, Mr Brownlee. Do you mean to let those tinkers settle here for the winter?"

"Yes, I do." Bristling a little now, the old man faced up to the sergeant. "Their kids have to do a hundred days' schooling a year, haven't they? That's the law, and you know it. And so what if I do let them settle here while the kids go to school?"

"Just this," the sergeant told him. "It's my opinion still that they're nothing but a lot of rogues, and they won't send their kids to school anyway. But if they don't, I'll have the authorities down on them. If they break the law in any way, in fact, any way at all, I'll be down on them so hard that they'll be glad to move on from here."

The old man stared at the sergeant, bewilderment in his look; and Constable Miller, too, could not help staring now. *Hadn't the sarge listened at all when Brownlee was talking? Didn't he realise what it meant when he spoke of making the travellers move on?* The old man spoke, the sound of his voice drawing the constable's gaze to him.

"But where to, sergeant? Where can they go if you make them move on?"

"That's their affair. So you're answered now, aren't you, Mr Brownlee?" With a nod, then, and a brisk, "Good day," the sergeant closed the interview; but once back in the patrol car he made no bones about telling Constable Miller that Mr Brownlee's part in it had shown him to be nothing more than a soft old fool.

"I suppose he is," Miller agreed; yet still, as he spoke, his conscience pricked him; and it was with rebellion against the sergeant in his mind that he thought of traveller families being forced to move on only to find that, for such as them, there was no resting-place.

"That sergeant," Rhona said, "the big chap that has it in for you, Cat – he's gunning for us. My Mammy says he told Mr Brownlee we'll do our hundred days' schooling, or he'll have the Cruelty on us."

"It's not the Cruelty they call it nowadays," Alec corrected her. "It's Welfare, or Social Services, or something like that."

"What difference does the name make?" Rhona argued. "We'll still have some bloke driving up to the camp and telling any of us that don't go to school, "You, there! Into the car!" Then off he'll go with whoever it is, and that one will end up in a Home."

"That one won't be me." Alec stretched out complacently on the grassy slope where they sat looking down towards Brownlee's farm. "I'll tell them I'm above school age – because I'm fourteen now, dammit. And look at that!" He flexed his long muscular legs and grinned at Rhona. "I look sixteen, don't I? And if I tell them I'm sixteen they'll just have to believe me."

"Ach, you!" Rhona gave Alec's legs an admiring glance that belied the reproach in her tone, and turned to Charlie. "How about you, Charlie? Will you risk the Cruelty?"

"I'll sign on at the school," Charlie said, "just to keep sweet with the Cruelty at first. But I'll still go with my Daddy and my brothers when they're doin' the rounds for scrap, and the Cruelty's goin' to have a job to catch up with me then."

"What about you, Cat?" Rhona leaned across Alec to ask her question, and Alec seized on this as an opportunity to twine her hand in his. "Are you feared of the Cruelty man?"

Cat shrugged. "As much as you are, I suppose. I'm not wanting to be put in a Home. *And* I'm not wanting my Daddy in jail just because I've skipped school. I'll go, same as you will. But I tell you one thing. There'd better not be any trouble when we do."

"Trouble?" Rhona looked puzzled. "From the kids,

you mean? Calling us 'tinks' and 'dirty thieves' and all that?"

"Away no!" Cat raised a small but hard-knuckled fist. "We can deal with that sort of thing! I mean the teachers. They're the bosses. And if they start trying to push us about – well, we'll just have to walk out of that school, won't we?"

Rhona pursed her lips and frowned a little at this. But Cat was right, of course. It wasn't the traveller way to battle out any problem with authority. The traveller way was to move on and leave the problem behind. And so that was just what she and Cat would have to do. All the same . . . Rhona cast a curious sideways glance at her cousin, noting again the difference in her from the Cat McPhie who had been so afraid of the two big polis striding into the camp in Wilson's Wood in the Spring of that year. Cat met her glance with the look of cool independence she had acquired since then, and Rhona said hastily:

"Aye, well. You're right. We'll just do that."

"Fine." Cat nodded. "So we know where we are now. But to tell you the truth, the only thing that really bothers me about going to school is not being able to take Shuffler with me."

Shuffler stirred at the mention of his name and turned his head towards Cat. His big frame had filled out in the course of the summer. Now he had his full adult weight, and there was a glisten on his smooth black hide that was like the glisten of jet. He had been gently panting as he lay and the turn of his head showed a half-open mouth lined with two rows of white and formidable-looking teeth.

Charlie and Alec looked respectfully at him, and then enviously at Cat. Rhona started to look disdainful, then thought better of doing so. Rhona still had a vivid memory of the stormy argument at the beginning of the potato harvest when she had jeered at Cat for being a split mechanic. And it was Cat who had won that argument – Cat, whose friendship she wanted so much to keep, who had managed to dictate the price of that friendship! Alec stretched a hand to fondle Shuffler's ears, and said:

"I wish he was mine."

The longing in his voice was intense; but Charlie was not yet so ready to admit that his envy of Cat had overcome his first reservations on her altered status. Dismissively he said:

"Ah, but he's maybe not so fast as Cat says he is. Or as strong."

"Ach, come on, Charlie!" Cat was smiling as she spoke, much amused by Charlie's last-ditch stand. "You've wrestled him. You know his strength. And I'm not saying he's as fast on the flat as some dogs – his build's too heavy for that – but you saw him bring down the hare that sprang out of Brownlee's corn stacks. And you couldn't ask any dog to turn and dodge quicker than he did, could you? Besides, I'll tell you something that shows how fast he is in another way." Her voice dropped a tone, and without her realising it, took on the very note of Old Nan's storytelling voice.

"You all know how easy it is to startle grouse out of the heather. They don't lie close, the way a blackcock does – so close you can be almost treading on it before it shoots upwards. And up north where we were this summer, one of the things that Shuffler learned from my daddy's Sheba, was the scent of blackcock."

Cat paused to glance around the other three – Rhona of the pale face and the sunset-coloured hair that showed

91

how the "red McPhies" had intermarried with the "black McPhies", Alec with the dark, aquiline features of the MacDonalds, Charlie with his ruddy-fair complexion burned even redder by the sun of the past summer. Rhona's pale cheek was laid close to Alec's dark one. Charlie's brow was furrowed with concentration. All three of them were silently willing her to continue.

"I've walked a moor with Shuffler," she told them, "and him scenting for blackcock. I've seen one rise in front of him, and I've seen him spring at the very second it rose – spring so fast that he caught that bird on the wing and brought it back to earth with him, stone-dead. Not once, either. Not twice, but quite a number of times. So now, Charlie – " With her eyes going directly to Charlie on the words, Cat finished, "What d'you say to that?"

Charlie leaned back on his elbow, his breath coming out in a long sigh. "Jeez!" he muttered. "Oh, jeez, Cat!" Turning on his side he began admiringly to stroke the glistening jet-black of Shuffler's hide. The dog lay quiet under his caress, and with a longing that was now undisguised, Charlie echoed Alec's wish. "I wish he was mine!"

"I thought you would," Cat told him; but she was generous in victory with no sneering in her voice, no triumph. And Charlie, it seemed, recognised that this was so. He smiled at her, and the smile told her that he no longer minded her being aware that he too had at last come to terms with the thought of her as she now was.

Just like her daddy had said he would, she reminded herself; that night beside Loch Ness, and all the other nights since then . . . With quiet pleasure in the knowledge that she had been accepted on her own terms among her

92

chosen friends, Cat sat looking downwards to the camp on Brownlee's farm; but it was only with the outward eye, now, that she saw this.

Inwardly, now, her vision had become filled again with the sight of silver water on a purple moor, with the giant grey castles of Ben Loyal and the changing colours of the Kyle of Tongue, with one picture after another of the small, hidden places Old Nan had promised them – little coves where the sand gleamed white, and seals basked, and Old Nan had told stories of mermaids ... Arms hugging her knees, Cat sighed a long sigh of regret and yearning. It hadn't been long, their stay in the enchanted land. And the road back had been a hard one!

Work at the tattie harvest had been hard too; but that, at least, was over now, and tonight there would be the celebration to mark the end of it. Still with only half an ear for the conversation of the other three beside her, Cat continued to let her mind drift; and now it was the camp that occupied her thoughts.

There was a big crowd of them gathered there that year – all the McPhies, Charlie's family, Alec's family, Joe Reid and his lot. The Reids had taken their time over going back to Ireland – and it wasn't as if they were popular, either, what with Morven making eyes at all the men, and that brat Moura just as bad as her mother! So which of the boys would Moura set her cap at that night when the celebration started? Because she would be sure to pick on one of them, of course – but there was something else that was equally sure. It wouldn't be Alec MacDonald that was snared by her dark eyes and her flashy gold earrings! Alec had always been sweet on Rhona; but now, it was plain, he was dead set on her. In traveller terms, in fact, he had "marked her down" for marriage. And as for Rhona, she would soon take care of any girl who tried to woo Alec away from her!

As if the thought had prompted the sound, there was a sudden yelp of protest from Rhona. The yelp turned into a laugh that chimed in with another laugh from Alec. Cat turned her head towards the noise and saw Alec teasing Rhona with a branch of gorse, bringing it just close enough to her bare leg to let the prickles scratch, then snatching it back before she could seize it from him.

Cat smiled at the horseplay, and a glance at Charlie showed that he too was smiling. But still, in spite of her amusement, there was something about the branch of gorse that nagged at her mind, something that wasn't involved with fooling around, that had to do with weeping instead of laughing, something . . . The elusive memory leapt suddenly into her mind.

There had been flowers on the gorse on the day of the cuckoo snow when Granda McPhie had died, tiny yellow flowers perched like brilliant little butterflies on the snow that crusted the gorse bushes. And she had wondered about that, because gorse was a summer flower. Yet here it was now, the month of October, and still there were flowers scattered on the branch of gorse in Alec's hand.

"It's strange," she said, "the way you can get flowers on gorse at any time of the year. Have you ever noticed that?"

Alec and Rhona looked blankly at her. But Charlie said, and grinned as he said it:

"I have. And that's why they say, *When gorse is out it's kissing-time.*"

"Charlie Drummond!" Rhona sat up straight, her pale and pretty face no longer smiling, but looking scandalised instead. "That's a thing for a man to say – not a laddie like you. You need your mouth washed out!"

"Do I?" Charlie also sat up straight, and glared angrily at Rhona. "Then you need your tongue clipped!"

"Hey, Charlie – " In dismay, Alec began protesting against Charlie's retort; but Charlie scrambled to his feet and began marching away down the slope. Alec continued to protest, Rhona continued to talk indignantly about "a laddie like him saying things like that." Cat said nothing, but she watched Charlie as he marched away and was struck by what she realised she was seeing in him.

Charlie had grown taller and broader in the summer just past. His shoulders had filled out. There was an agressive male swagger about the way he carried himself. And so Rhona was wrong. Charlie wasn't any longer "a laddie." Charlie was now more than half-way to being a man; and one part of her was sorry about that and the fact that it meant the end of a childhood friendship, but there was still another part that was glad of it and was enjoying the strange sort of excitement the gladness brought to her.

"If you do move on," the man said, "where will you go?"

Cat and Rhona glanced at one another. Let the man say what he like, the glances conveyed, the decision had been taken even before the start of all the trouble with that biology teacher insisting they would attend her classes. And since they were both determined not to do that – either at her command *or* the Headmaster's – there had been no choice except to walk out of school.

But that couldn't be the end of it, of course; not with Sergeant McKendrick waiting to make his pounce on them and their daddies. And so once again what choice did they have – all of them now – except to move on to some other winter camp? Rhona pressed closer to Cat.

Both girls edged nearer to Cat's mother and Rhona's mother. Charlie's mother and Alec's mother closed ranks with the girls and the other women until all of them were in a solid phalanx behind Old Nan and all of them facing the man who had put the question to them.

"Where *will* you go?" he asked again. "Because you know even better than I do that it's getting more and more difficult for travellers to find camp sites – especially when it comes to long-stay winter camps."

Old Nan looked stolidly at him before she answered for all of them – for the men-folk as well as for the women, although the men would be equally affected by what she had to say. But even so, the root of the trouble with Cat and Rhona was strictly women's business; and she was well aware, therefore, that the absent men would agree with any judgement she had to make on it.

"According to you," she observed, "you're a doctor – name of Ballantyne. But we don't hold with doctors. That's not our way. And what I want to know is the reason that brought you here in the first place."

"I'm not a medical doctor, Mrs McPhie. I'm a doctor of philosophy. And if you'll just listen – "

"Listen, is it?" Vehemently Old Nan interrupted. "This is women's business, and you've less than no right to be talking of it to us if you're not even a proper doctor."

"But I'm here because I want to help you." The man, Dr Ballantyne, made a pleading little gesture with his hands. "I'm here because I'm part of an official project that takes an interest in travellers. The Headmaster of the girls' school knows that, or he'd have left it all to the Social Services instead of asking me to talk to you."

"Would he now!" Old Nan's tone was no less hostile.

than before. "And what makes you think your 'official project' is any more welcome than those damn snoopers in the Cruelty?"

Dr Ballantyne smiled a rueful little smile. "You don't hold with officials either, I see. But I don't blame you for that. I don't hold with them myself. And I don't want to snoop on you or ask you to fill in forms or anything like that. Because it just so happens, you see, that I like travellers. All I want is to do something that'll help them get a square deal from people who don't sympathise with their way of life. And so, as far as my part in the project is concerned, I'd rather you looked on me as a friend instead of as an official."

Old Nan continued to stare steadily at him. The women and girls grouped behind her stared also. The man was short and balding. His expression was kindly. His eyes were not those of a man who told lies. Grudgingly, Old Nan said:

"Aye, well. But if you know travellers you'll know too that Cat and Rhona had good reason for leaving that school. Our girls, my mannie, are brought up to be modest creatures."

"Agreed. And very necessary too, when you have different generations sharing cramped sleeping quarters. I'm with you all the way there."

"Well, then – " Old Nan was now half-way to triumph. "Modesty is the last thing you'll get in those – those – " Confused for a moment she turned to Rhona. "What did you call them, hen?"

"Biology classes," Rhona whispered.

"Aye." Old Nan nodded, and then almost spat the word out at Dr Ballantyne, "*biology* classes, with pictures of naked men and women on the walls, and that woman

97

teacher – ashamed of herself she should be – ranting on to boys and girls together about things that are only for married folk to know."

Cat and Rhona stole another quick glance at one another; and in the scarlet colour in Rhona's face Cat saw reflected her own blush of embarrassment – that same awful embarrassment that had gripped them both in the moment of first hearing the biology teacher so brazenly trumpeting aloud of things they had always been taught were private matters – woman-talk, mother and daughter secrets. And all those boys – stranger boys at that! – sitting alongside them with ears fairly flapping as they took it all in!

"Look, Mrs McPhie." Dr Ballantyne glanced from Old Nan to the women all nodding agreement with her remarks, and seemed to gather himself for a last attempt at argument. "If Rhona and Cat don't do their hundred days at school, you've got two options. Either you all run away or the Social Services will come down on the girls and the police will be after their fathers."

"We'll run." Old Nan put on her most stoic face. "It won't be the first time."

"But if you listen to me," Dr Ballantyne persisted, "you could have a third option. I'll strike a bargain with you. You make sure the girls go back to school, and in return, I'll guarantee to persuade the Headmaster to excuse them from attending the biology classes. Now – " He paused for a moment as if to allow for time to let his words sink in. "How does that appeal to you?"

Old Nan held his gaze for a long moment, then turned to whisper to her guardian phalanx of mothers. The whispering at an end, she turned back to Dr Ballantyne and asked him:

"Have we your word on that?"

"My solemn word. The Headmaster doesn't want to get involved with the Social Services people. I know he doesn't. And he wants even less to have any trouble from that big Sergeant McKendrick. Between you and me, in fact, he can't stand the Sergeant. And he's not a hard man in himself, either, so that he'd be quite agreeable to arranging alternative classes for Cat and Rhona. And that way, you see, they'll get all the education that's needed to satisfy the law."

Once more, before she made any answer to this, Old Nan consulted the other women. "Right!" She turned from them to whisper to Cat and Rhona, and when she had their agreement also, was ready for Dr Ballantyne. "That's fine by us – including the lassies. Although I can tell you this, my mannie. All they'll ever need to be taught, their mammies will teach them. Because it's only traveller skills they'll ever use, you see. And it's God's truth I speak now, if they have these skills and their mammies and daddies to love them, they'll be happier bairns than any school could make them."

Dr Ballantyne sighed. "I'll not argue with you on that, Mrs McPhie. It's not my place to decide such things. But so long as we've reached agreement in this particular instance . . . "

With a shrug that showed he thought there was nothing more to say, Dr Ballantyne sketched a small bow of farewell, but then was seemingly struck by some further thought. He slid a hand into an inside pocket of his jacket, drew out a small, printed card, and handed it to Old Nan.

"The times have changed, Mrs McPhie," he said, "just the way the situation about traditional traveller sites has changed; and it may be that some of you will have further need of a friend among those officials that you and I don't hold with. You can contact me at the address on that card. Or by phone. And I'll be glad to do what I can to help any of you. But especially, I'll be glad to help any of your youngsters."

With another small bow and a smile cast in Cat and Rhona's direction, he turned finally away. Old Nan glanced briefly at the card in her hand, and would have torn it across if Rhona had not exclaimed:

"Aw, come on, Nan! Just because you can't read . . . "

Deftly she took the card from Old Nan, turned it over curiously in her own hand, and studied the printing on the face of it."

"Let me see," Cat begged. Rhona showed her the card, and she glanced at the face of it before she took it from Rhona's fingers to study the printing for herself. A name, an address, a telephone number – maybe they would need these yet if there was any further trouble for herself and Rhona – *Rhona!*

Like a light bursting in her mind the knowledge broke on Cat that it was for Rhona's sake they would need to keep the information on the card – Rhona lying white and still in some hushed white place that smelt of death . . . The everyday sound of Old Nan's voice came to her, breaking into that awful moment of enlightenment, banishing this latest manifestation of the gift she had inherited.

"Well, you've seen what you wanted to see. So what will you do now with his fancy wee bit cardboard?"

Cat looked at Rhona, but Rhona only shrugged as if she had lost all interest in the card.

"I'll keep it, I think." With her tone as casual as the

100

turmoil in her mind would allow, Cat slipped the card into a pocket of the jeans she had bought with her share of the potato harvest money.

"And what good d'you think it's going to do you, keeping that?"

"I dunno." Still making a great effort to be casual, Cat turned away from the old woman. "But I'll tell you, won't I, if I think its going to come in handy?"

"Aye, if I'm still here to see the day," Old Nan grumbled; and with a hand sliding down into her pocket to touch the card again, Cat hoped fervently that she would indeed be there still when the thing that the gift had foretold came true.

7

It was summer again, a morning of the summer four years on from the one of the journey north with Old Nan. But Old Nan was dead now. Old Nan was only a pleasant, smiling ghost at the camp fire where her stories were remembered and retold to the children who had not heard them before.

And Pibroch, too, was dead. The grey, steady presence of Pibroch had been replaced by a battered old car coughing its unreliable way along routes that modern roadworks had changed out of all recognition from the ones he had travelled. Instead of the cart he had so faithfully pulled, there was a trailer as battered as the car. And both car and trailer now were part of the camp where travellers had settled for a few weeks of the summer to earn money at picking raspberries.

It was the right weather, too, for that kind of work – a bright, warm day, with no threat of the rain that would make the berries too soft to pick, or cause them to rot on the bush. The workers were out in force, with local pickers among them as well as travellers; but Cat McPhie, that morning, had more on her mind than picking rasps. Cat was at the farmhouse overlooking the raspberry fields, and she was in the process of trying to rescue Shuffler from what looked like certain death.

The door of the farmhouse gaped wide open. Framed in the doorway stood a man with a shotgun raised in the firing position. The gun was pointed at Shuffler; and Shuffler, although he knew about guns and was well aware of the threat in this one, was not trying to run from it. Tail down, and whining miserably, he held his ground at point blank range of the gun's muzzle, and it was only Cat rushing to stand in front of him that saved him from the shot.

"No!" Cat screamed as she ran. "Don't do it, Mr Ross, please don't do it!"

Slowly, with a look of disgust on his face, the farmer, Ross, lowered his gun. His voice rough with frustrated anger, he told Cat:

"I warned you, didn't I? Twice before I've warned you. That dog's a bloody nuisance, haunting the house the way it does, scratching the door, whining to get in."

Cat held back the retort she would have liked to make. *And what else d'you expect, with that collie bitch of yours in heat, and her scent driving him mad to get at her?* Humbly, instead, she answered:

"I know, Mr Ross. And I'm very sorry. But he won't get away from me again, I promise you. Not with this around his neck!"

Quickly she made a running noose from the steel choke chain she had fished out of her pocket and dropped the noose over Shuffler's head. She pulled the noose tight around Shuffler's neck; and, grudgingly, the farmer said:

"Well, you're trying at least. But it's his last chance, mind. And mind you too, that I've a right to shoot any dog that's a nuisance on my property, so don't come bawling to me if you find this damn beast of yours dead on the rubbish tip."

"No, sir. Thank you, sir," Cat agreed. But she was speaking to the farmer's back by this time; and with a tug on the ring at the free end of the choke chain, she told Shuffler:

"Come on, then, you daft gomeril."

Grim-faced she started back to the camp, a small figure still in spite of her added years, but with her childhood sturdiness now refined to a lean and whiplike strength that could jerk the choke chain tight whenever Shuffler tried to resist her pull on it. They reached the camp and the evidence of her past failures to stop Shuffler's attempts to get near the collie bitch.

Hammered well into the ground beside the trailer was an iron stake. Beside it was the leather collar he had worked up and over his head, the leather thongs he had chewed through to make his second bid for freedom. But this time would be different. With the choke chain becoming tighter around his neck the more he pulled against it, and the choke linked to the stake with that heavy length of iron chain her father had found for her –

"Now then!" With a final look of appraisal at her finished work, she stepped back from the tethered dog. "Let's see you get away now, my lad!" Shuffler whined and lunged towards her, then gasped as the choke chain cut off his breath. He backed till the chain slackened enough to let him breathe normally. "Aye, you're learning!" Quickly, refusing to let herself see the pleading in Shuffler's eyes, Cat pushed a dish of water well within his reach, and began running towards the raspberry fields.

There was quite a crowd around the truck where she collected her basket for picking – all of them young men who jostled one another and laughed hoarsely as she neared the truck. One of them, a fellow with a shock of yellow hair, said jeeringly:

"Doin' anything tonight, dearie?"

Cat reached for her basket, ignoring him. From across the truck, her eyes met those of a young man wearing a shirt that hung open to show a mass of chest hair. He grinned at her, and started to speak:

" 'Cos if you're not – " His eyes roved over her, and came brazenly to rest on the vee of her open-necked blouse.

These two, Cat realised, were neither locals nor travellers. Locals would have had the sense to leave a traveller girl alone. Travellers would never offend against their own code by addressing such talk or such looks to a traveller girl. These two were the scrapings of some city back street – the kind who sometimes appeared at the berries for nothing more than the chance to loaf in the sun and get drunk on any money that came their way.

"Yobbos", the locals would have called them; but she could sense something evil in their loutishness, something that brought to her mind the traveller words for "bad men." *Shan gadgies* – that's what these two were! Disgustedly she told them:

"That'll be the day when I go out wi' the likes o' you yobbos. I've seen better scum on a sewage pond."

Without waiting to see the reaction to this she turned swiftly away towards the raspberry fields, and glanced along the rows of bushes till she found the one where her mother was picking.

"Shuffler?" Ilsa looked up at Cat's approach. "Did you get him?"

"Aye. And chained him up, too, just the way my Daddy told me."

Ilsa nodded approval, then smiled a little as she said, "You missed seeing Charlie Drummond. It's not ten

108

minutes since he was here, looking for you."

"Oh?" Cat began picking raspberries, her fingers flying to make up for lost time. "What brought Charlie here?"

"Maybe he just wanted to see you. I don't know. But what he said he wanted was Shuffler."

"That's no surprise. Charlie's always envied me that dog. So what's special today about wanting him?"

"Just this, it seems." Ilsa paused to wipe sweat off her brow. "Daddler Drummond has finally taken the plunge and bought himself that scrap yard he had his eye on. So now he's after a guard dog for the yard."

"And Charlie thinks he can get Shuffler for that?"

"That's the idea. He knows the trouble you're having to keep the creature away from the farmer's bitch; and so, he says, he's willing to take him off your hands for a job where there won't be that sort of bother. He'll come back later this morning to see if you'll agree to that."

"Will he so?" In silent anger, Cat began to rehearse what she would have to tell Charlie on his return. Her dog, a creature that had always lived as free as herself to be shut up in a compound full of scrap metal, never again to feel grass under his feet or to smell the wind except for the scent of some thieving yobbo or other, and taught – yes *taught* – to rage at everyone except Charlie Drummond himself . . . *Oh, Charlie, Charlie! How could you ever think I'd agree to that!*

Ilsa had nothing further to say, it seemed, once she had given the news about Charlie, and the two of them continued picking in silence, with Cat's anger only gradually abating enough to let her begin looking around for a sight of familiar faces among the rows of raspberry bushes. Rhona was there, she saw then. There was no mistaking the sight of that red head bobbing up and down among the dark green of the raspberry foliage. And Alec was with her. He was so much taller than the bushes that she could see him clearly, with his dark head never far away from Rhona's shining red one.

Love birds! That's what they were. Always trying to keep as close to one another as possible, even after a year of marriage! Cat smiled at the thought, forgetting Charlie altogether in the pleasure of it, then began to wonder how long it would be before Rhona and Alec set out to travel on their own, instead of with Alec's parents. Not until a good while after Rhona's baby was born, she reckoned – because that was always the tradition, after all, for the young married ones to travel with the boy's parents until his mother was sure the girl could look after babies on her own. And Rhona, of course, would be the very last one to break with tradition!

The train of thought that had brought to mind the baby so soon to be born to Rhona reminded Cat also that her mother, too, was now pregnant again. And although there probably wasn't any more chance of survival for this baby that there had been for the other ones, still . . .

"Mammy – " With a sense of responsibility beginning to nag at her, Cat turned to her mother. "It's going to be a hot day, this, a real scorcher. It's too hot already, in fact, for you to be working. D'you think – "

She stopped, feeling the question interrupted by the smile Ilsa turned on her.

"You're not to worry, Cat." Her mother's voice was soft, as always. "I know how things will be this time. I have the gift, remember. Same as you."

Same as you. Cat returned to her picking, an odd sort of resentment running through the questions Ilsa's words had raised in her mind. This business of having the gift, it

110

was something strange, something she didn't really like to think about. And what did her mother mean, anyway – *I know how things will be this time*. Was she resigned already to losing this baby the way she had lost all the others? Or could it be that she was not only hoping this one would survive, but actually sure that it would?

Furtively, from that time, she watched her mother, wondering often at the air of serenity on Ilsa's face, constantly watchful of some possible collapse. But it was she herself who began to droop before Ilsa did, and it was Ilsa, eventually, who said:

"Tell you what, Cat. We've picked enough for a wage today, both of us. I'll away and make a cup of tea. You take a dander up the river where it's cool and see if your Daddy's had any luck at the pearling, and I'll just sit in the shade till you both come back. Eh, now? How does that strike you?"

"Like a good idea," Cat confessed. "But I'll carry the baskets to the truck, Mammy. You just go on and lift the kettle. That'll be heavy enough for you."

Thankfully then, as Ilsa walked off towards the trailer, she began carrying the baskets to the truck where they would be weighed and the amount of wages due would be marked up on the tally-sticks.

"Had enough?" The two yobbos who had accosted her earlier – he of the yellow hair and he of the hairy chest – were still there, with nothing better to do apparently than give some vague assistance to the tally man. It was Yellowhair who spoke to her, with Hairy-chest looking on and grinning the same insolent grin as before; but she turned her back on them and stared towards the river running into the woods beyond the fruit farm, until eventually the tally man's shout released her to start walking in the direction of her stare.

It was cooler by the river than in the raspberry fields, but there was no sign of her father on the flat stretch where the best mussel beds were to be found. He must have gone upriver, Cat decided, past the series of waterfalls that brought it down from the high ground of the moor beyond, and wondered if she should bother going that far. But suppose he had found a pearl, a really good one, and was dying to tell her about it?

Excited at the thought moving in her, she began to climb the steep zigzag of path leading past the waterfalls; but ten minutes of this exertion made her as hot as she had been before, with sweat rolling down to paste the thin stuff of her blouse to her and dampening her jeans so that they chafed uncomfortably against her legs. The sound of the river was tormenting her, too, the sound of water rushing – cool water, cool, cool, cool . . . Like it had used to be when she swam with Shuffler, she thought longingly, and stopped to stare across the amber-coloured width of a pool at the foot of a waterfall.

The pool lay at a bend of the river – a basin of still water with rapids above it and rapids below. The water that fed it poured in a mad cataract of white over the lip of the high parapet of rock that formed the further curve of the basin. But the nearer curve of the basin, where Cat stood, was a flat, grassy bank, only two feet above the sun-flecked amber of the water.

With her gaze swiftly taking all this in, her mind unconsciously computing the distance she had come from the raspberry farm, Cat moved to the edge of the grassy bank. Standing there, she turned her head to listen. No sound except the rushing of the waterfall! Her gaze swept around, intently scanning the green and the dapple of sunlight that was the wood. No movement there, no least sign of any presence!

Her eyes came back to the pool. It would be deep, she reckoned, with that amount of water falling constantly into it. And she didn't have Shuffler with her – but then, of course, she didn't need Shuffler now that she could swim. By this time, too, she must have walked at least half a mile upriver, and so she was probably half as far again from the farm and the people there.

The longing to feel the coolness close to her became irresistible. In a few quick movements she had kicked off her shoes, stripped off her clothes, and was plunging into the water, gasping as it hit her, choking and gasping with delight and exhilaration. But not yelling, she admonished herself as she felt again the instinct to release her feelings the way she had used to do on such occasions. Sound carried, after all, especially in the clear air of such a day as this was, and it would be foolish to risk the yell she would so dearly have loved to let loose.

Smiling, she swam a few lazy strokes across the pool, and turned when she felt the dangerous undertow from the waterfall. She ducked and somersaulted, feeling the water as smooth and sensuous against her skin as it had always been in those days when she swam with Shuffler. The thought flashed through her mind that it was from him she had learned to beware the undertow from a waterfall. She surfaced, smiling again at this thought, and saw them standing on the bank – the two yobbos from the fruit farm, the *shan gadgies!*

8

Blinding panic hit Cat. The yobbos were waving to her and hoarsely shouting, while Yellowhead clutched a bundle of her clothes and Hairychest flourished her shoes. She screamed at them to put her things down, to go away, to leave her alone. For answer, they tossed her clothes and shoes away into the wood and yelled to her to come and get them back. Then Yellowhead came close to the edge of the water.

"Thought you were smart, eh?" he bellowed. "callin' us 'scum'. Didn't think we'd get you for that, did you? But we have now, see? We followed you, and now you're goin' to pay for givin' us lip."

"And how!" Hairychest had followed Yellowhead to shout agreement with him. In obscene detail then, the two of them began to yell of the things they would do to her to make her pay; and coldly through her panic came the realisation that there was nothing she could do to avoid the revenge they had in mind.

There was no way out of the pool except by means of that grassy bank; but even if there had been, the camp was nearly a mile away. And even if she had been prepared to run naked for nearly a mile, how could she possibly hope to outdistance two men? There wasn't even a hope of rescue, either – not with her mother being the only one to know where she had gone and her father not due back for hours yet, from the pearling!

But she wouldn't beg, she told herself fiercely, she wouldn't beg that filthy pair for mercy; and all the time he shouts of obscenity continued to ring out around her, kept desperately paddling and treading water in a sort of forlorn hope that they might tire of their dirty game.

"Come out!" Yellowhead bellowed eventually. " 'Cos f you don't we'll come and get ya!"

If I don't drown first! In panic again as the knowledge of her rapidly-tiring limbs sent the thought flashing through her head, Cat finally succumbed and sought the mercy she had vowed she would never beg.

"Please! Oh, please leave me alone. Please go away."

"Please, oh please!" they jeered, and launched into a grotesque game of patacake, each slapping the other's hands and mockingly chanting, *My mother told me/I never should/Play with the gypsies/In the wood.*

Cat felt water washing into her mouth; and with that came the sickening realisation that she had been right in thinking she would not be able to keep afloat for much longer. And she had no Shuffler to hold on to now – poor Shuffler chained to his stake . . . An idea pierced the despair in her mind – a mad idea! A dog's hearing was a hundred times more acute than a human's, wasn't it? Supposing she whistled to Shuffler! Was there a chance he might hear her, even at that distance, and kick up enough commotion to warn her mother she was in trouble?

With difficulty she raised one of her tired and heavy arms above the water, and put her fingers into her mouth for the most ear-splitting whistle she could summon. The sound came out flat, weak, useless; but even so, in the instant that followed her failure, she heard Shuffler bark. Or had she? The water was washing into her mouth again, her head was sinking back, arms and legs becoming

115

too heavy to move . . . The bark again − or was it all just part of the nightmare of drowning?

Yellowhead galvanised her into a last despairing effort at keeping touch with life. Yellowhead advanced to the very edge of the bank, and shouted:

"All right then, seein' you won't come out, now we *are* comin' to get you!"

"*Shuffler!*" Thrusting head and shoulders clear of the water, Cat yelled, and yelled again, "*SHUFFLER!*"

He came bounding out of the woods, teeth a flash of white in his snarling jaws, powerful shoulder muscles impelling him urgently forward. Again she shouted, an arm outflung to point at Yellowhead.

"Seize him! *Seize!*"

Yellowhead glanced back over his shoulder in time to see Shuffler in mid-leap towards him. He spun round, bellowing his alarm, arms thrown up to protect his face. Shuffler's jaws closed around his right forearm; and man and dog went crashing to the ground.

Hairychest started forward to the thrashing mass of human and canine limbs, made as if to kick Shuffler, and apparently decided instead to save his own skin. He turned to run into the woods, and ran straight into Charlie Drummond − Charlie with his broad shoulders flexed as he swung the heavy iron chain that had fixed Shuffler to his stake.

Somehow, as a medley of shouting and cursing was added to the screams of pain from Yellowhead, Cat managed to get as far as the edge of the bank. Charlie and Hairychest were no longer in sight by then; but Shuffler still had Yellowhead pinned to the ground with a grip that was fierce enough to send blood from the man's forearm oozing up around his jaws. But Yellowhead was at least

116

doing the right thing now by lying still instead of struggling against the dog's grip, and his screaming had died away into whimpers of pain.

Weakly she gave the command that made Shuffler release him; and clung to the bank's edge as he blundered off into the woods, nursing his injured arm and still whimpering. Shuffer came to nose down at her. He licked her face, streaming now with tears as well as river water, and cocked his ears in puzzlement at the salty taste of the tears.

She got one hand up and twined in the choke chain still around his neck. With the other hand she grasped a tussock of grass. Shuffler jerked his head in protest against the tightening of the chain. He backed away from her; but she hung on to the chain, and his movement created just enough pull to bring her up over the edge of the bank.

Between her grip on the grass, then, and the dog's still-determined resistance to the constriction of the chain, she managed to inch, and wriggle, and scramble, till she was lying flat out on the bank. Her hand dropped away from the chain. Slowly she brought her knees up and began to crawl towards a big old tree with spreading roots that bulged out of the ground at its base. She reached the hollows created by the roots and crouched into one of these hollows, crouched well down below the roots on either side of her, drawing her knees up, crossed arms hugging her body, making herself as small as she could – smaller, smaller yet, small as a baby not yet born . . .

Shuffler came to sit in front of her, head cocked to one side in question, his eyes anxious, but she was in such a hysteria of shivering and weeping that she was hardly aware of his presence. Something dropped down suddenly to cover her nakedness – a man's jacket. Suddenly too, there was another presence beside that of Shuffler – Charlie, standing with the length of chain swinging from his hand. And there was blood on the chain, and Charlie was speaking, angrily speaking in words that she had somehow, somewhere, heard him say before then.

"You've shamed me, Cat McPhie. You've put terrible shame on me."

She closed her eyes and huddled the jacket closer to her. The warmth of it began to spread through her. Her taut muscles relaxed a little, so that she shivered less. Her sobbing eased till there were no longer tears flowing from under her closed eyelids. She became aware of a noise close at hand – the sound of feet trampling the under-growth of the wood. Her eyes flew open in a swift, renewed access of terror.

Charlie wasn't there. Charlie was no longer beside her. And Shuffler wasn't there either! Then she saw them both coming out of the woods towards her, and the coldness of the terror was banished in a warm flood of relief. It was them she had heard trampling around in the bushes!

Charlie had left her in order to search for her clothes, she realised. He was holding them bundled up in front of him now, with her shoes lying on top of them.

"Here." He dropped the bundle in front of her. "Get dressed. I'll wait till you're ready."

He turned and walked from her, to stand looking out across the pool. She reached a hand towards her clothes and began slowly, very slowly, to get dressed. The clothes stuck to her damp skin. Her fingers shook, so that she was awkward with fastenings. She began to wonder how Charlie could have the patience to stand there for so long, unmoving, while she fumbled and struggled. She reached for his jacket when she was finished at last, drew it over her again, and called uncertainly:

"I'm ready, Charlie."

Charlie turned away from the river, walked to the tree and sat down beside her. Shuffler lay down in his usual position, his chin resting on her feet. She waited for Charlie to speak, but it was a long time before he did so, and then his voice was gloomy.

"These two," he said, "the one that Shuffler chewed up and the one I bashed with the chain, they'll be back at the farm before long. And they'll tell everybody what you did – swimming here as naked as the day you were born."

"But they'll not go back to the farm." Startled, she turned to stare at Charlie. "They couldn't, Charlie. They couldn't go back and talk about me like that. Not without giving themselves away – how they followed me here, and spied on me. And my daddy would kill them for that. You know he would – and they know it too. What's more, he'd make them admit what they meant to do to me if you hadn't come along. And there isn't a traveller man that wouldn't help my daddy then, to kill them."

"All right, so they won't go telling tales at the farm. But they'll still go to the polis with their story. One with his arm chewed up, the other with his head split open, they'll go to the polis and complain – tell lies that it was me attacked them for no reason at all. Then the polis will be at the camp with their questions; and so it'll still have to come out about you swimming here."

"No, no!" Vehemently Cat shook her head. "They'll not go to the polis, those two. I mean, just think, Charlie. *Shan gadgies* like them, they're bound to have a record as

119

long's your arm. They'll steer clear o' the polis – well clear of them, believe me."

"You're damn sure of yourself, aren't you?" Charlie looked sourly at her. "But it doesn't change what you did. Doesn't make a damn bit o' difference to that, does it?"

With scarlet rushing up into her face, Cat turned away from his look. Because he was right, of course. He had saved her from the worst those two men could have done to her, but she had still done what no traveller girl should ever do. She had allowed herself to be seen naked – not just by one strange man, either, but by two of them. The hysteria that had passed from her threatened to take hold again; and suddenly again, she felt so weak and shivery! Head down and in silence, she let time go by; and Charlie too, was silent, until finally she ventured to say:

"But it'll not be so bad, will it, if nobody ever knows about it?"

"I'll know." Charlie spoke heavily, his voice full of grating anger. "And I'm the one that matters. I said you'd shamed me, and by God you have!"

The tone of his voice struck an answering spark of anger out of Cat; and in the sudden awakening of this feeling, her weakness vanished.

"Why you?" she demanded. "Just you tell me, Charlie Drummond. Why you more than anybody else?"

"You must be thick!" Charlie looked at her, shaking his head in disbelief. "Honest, Cat, you must be thick as two planks. And if you don't know, you must be the only one that doesn't. Because I've made it plain enough this while past, haven't I?"

"Made what plain? What're you bletherin' about. And why should it mean that you're the one I've shamed?"

120

Charlie leaned forward till his face was only inches from her own. "Because I've marked you down, that's why. Because it's me, Charlie Drummond, that you're goin' to marry. Because I'm your man, and it's shame on me that any other man should see my woman the way these two saw you!"

He was panting, his breath moist on her face, and his anger was such that she more than half-expected him to strike her. Instead, he drew back from her, letting the fist he had begun to raise drop back to his side. He looked away from her, and in the silence that fell between them, she had time to wonder how she felt about what he had said.

I've marked you down. It's me you're goin' to marry. Why hadn't she realised that, instead of just taking it for granted that Charlie was simply fond of her the way he had always been? And why had she never stopped to think beyond the fact that she had always been fond of Charlie? Very fond indeed, she realised, now that she had been forced to stop and think about it. But did that mean that she should agree to marry him – because there would be problems to be solved, wouldn't there, if she did agree? She spoke at last, quietly.

"I'm sorry you've been shamed, Charlie." He nodded, not looking at her; after a moment she went on. "But – about marrying you, I'll need time to think that over."

Again that nod, with his face turned away from her. She began to rise, feeling her legs weak at first. Charlie also rose, and gave her a steadying hand, then let her stamp about a bit till the strength was back in her legs. Shuffler began to prance around her, and this reminded her of Charlie's message about him. With a nod towards the dog, she said:

121

"My mammy told me you'd be back to see about him. Was that when you decided – " She hesitated, and Charlie finished for her:

"To follow you up the river path. Your Mammy said that's where you would be, and I took Shuffler along just so he could be off the chain for a while."

"Lucky you did. And Charlie, I'm awful grateful to you for saving me, but – " Again she hesitated, even more awkwardly this time, then forced herself to go on, "but you can't have him, Charlie. Not for any reason, but especially not for a guard dog in a scrapyard."

Unexpectedly then, Charlie smiled. "I wouldn't have used him for that. It was only a ploy to get him from you."

"Huh!" Cat found herself smiling in reply. "Your ploys won't work with me, Charlie. Not that one or any other!"

"We'll see," Charlie told her; and now he was no longer smiling. "I'll grant you the one about Shuffler. But for the rest, Cat, we'll see." He held out his hand to her. "Now give me my jacket and we'll go back to the camp just like nothing had happened. And if you breathe a word to a soul about what did happen – if you even tell your Mammy or your Daddy about it – you'll have me to reckon with. And you won't like that."

9

They would spend the rest of the summer pearling, Jim
McPhie announced when the raspberry season was
finished, and he had picked out a specially good spot for
that. The river wasn't a well-known one, and therefore
almost fished out, like the one he had been on. They
would be only a few miles from a small market town
where they could buy supplies; but even more importantly,
the town had a hospital he could reach quickly with Ilsa
when her labour started.

"And I'll join in the pearling!" With much satisfaction
in this thought, Cat surveyed the stretch of river her
father had chosen, and went with him on his first
prospecting stroll along the bank, while Ilsa unpacked at
the new camp.

The water was at the right level for fishing – just low
enough to let the mussel beds be seen below the surface;
and among the shells there was a fair number of old and
gnarled ones – the "crookbacks" that were those most
likely to contain a pearl. Cat said cheerfully:

"So we've a chance here of finding that one really good
pearl you're always hoping for. And then our fortune'll
be made, won't it?"

"Not *our* fortune, lassie." Gravely Jim reproved her.
"If we do have that kind of find it'll all be for him – the
bairn back there." He gestured over his shoulder to where
they had left Ilsa in the trailer; and with dismay, Cat

realised how his mind was working.

Ilsa's baby, this time, would live. It had to, after all the disappointments there had been. That was what he was willing himself to believe. Yet how could he do so when it was still impossible to tell what Ilsa herself thought about the baby's chances? And even supposing it did live, how could he be sure it would be the boy he had so long wanted?

"We'd better get fishing then," she said, and wondered as they turned back to the camp for their gear, if her voice had given away anything of the apprehension she felt for her father and the terrible blow he might yet have to endure.

The first two weeks of the pearling went by with only a few small pearls to show for it. But even these, they all knew, were saleable; and so there was no objection forthcoming when Cat decided to take a day off to visit the Game Fair that was held every August in the grounds of the big estate bordering on the town. She had worked as hard as her father had done, after all, standing all day and every day in cold and thigh-deep water; and so, with Shuffler at heel, she set off jauntily for her day at the Game Fair.

Outside the entrance to the estate, she slipped the choke chain around Shuffler's neck and linked the chain to a piece of strong cord. There would be shooting men at the Game Fair, gamekeepers and landed gentry and the like, all of them with their pedigreed spaniels and labradors and pointers; and if her Shuffler, her beloved mongrel got in among any of the pure-bred bitches there –

With an inward laugh at the thought, she paid her entrance money; and for almost two hours after that she enjoyed herself to the full, trying her hand at the fly-fishing and the archery, laughing herself silly at the terriers' race, wandering among the rows of stalls displaying all the kinds of orthodox sporting gear she would never use – not a poacher like her! – all the kinds of wet-weather gear she could never afford to buy, but still gravely trying to assess the merits of each item.

Deliberately also, she kept the shooting gallery to the last, because it was on the air-rifles there that she was determined to spend the little money she had. Not that she had ever used one before, of course – even so small and light a gun being something that no poacher like her would dare to be caught with. Yet still, she had always had the feeling that she could put up a good show with an air-rifle. And to her delight, the feeling proved to have been justified.

She shot well – so well in fact, that she was eventually one of the only two left in the shooting gallery's target competition.

"You're a natural, lassie," the gallery attendant remarked, and gallantly broke the gun open for her when it came to the start of the competition's last round.

"Thanks, mister." Flushed with pleasure, Cat took the gun – and then remembered. Each round had to be paid for before shooting started. And she had no money left. With disappointment making her flush even deeper, she glanced from the attendant to the one other competitor for the prize.

"I'm sorry, mister," she told the attendant, and handed the gun back to him. "I can't shoot again. My money's finished."

For a moment, the attendant looked blank, and the other competitor spoke into his silence. "Then it's mine, the prize. I've got one more point than she has, and if she doesn't go the last round, the prize must be mine."

Cat made to turn away so that she could release Shuffler from the post to which she had tied him while she shot; but now it was the attendant's turn to speak, quickly, and with some annoyance in his voice.

"Hold hard!" Cat looked back at him and saw that he was once more offering her the gun. "On the house," he said. "For you, hen, this last round is on the house."

Quickly she glanced from the gun to the other competitor – a tall, thin man in gamekeeper's tweeds. He was scowling, anger glinting out of the eyes close-set above his narrow nose; and suddenly, as clearly as if he had spoken, she knew the real reason for his anger.

The prize itself didn't matter to him. The prize was simply the winner's right to pick anything at all out of all the toys and china ornaments that made up the stock of the stall. And what would he want with any of these things?

Nothing, she realised. What mattered to him was that he was a gamekeeper, a man who used a gun every day of his life as a tool of his trade. Yet here he was in danger of being outshot by some chit of a girl, and his pride wasn't going to stand for that! But it would have to, she told herself grimly. It would damn well have to! Her hand reached out for the gun. The gallery attendant nodded encouragement to her, and she settle down to shoot.

There were six shots in the round. With the first one, she evened the score. On the next two shots, she and the gamekeeper pegged level for points. She curled a finger around the trigger for the fourth shot, and in the very moment of firing, felt something jog her elbow. Her shot went wide of the target. There was a surprised murmur from the ring of spectators that had formed around the gallery. The attendant looked sharply at her opponent.

"Mister," he said, "I saw that. I saw you jog her elbow."

"It was an accident." The gamekeeper was seemingly very busy reloading his gun and he answered sullenly, not looking at anyone.

"Too bad." The attendant's voice had a note of contempt in it. "But it cancels the shot, of course." He nodded to Cat. "Try again, lassie."

Her fourth shot was a bull. The gamekeeper scored an inner, and so now it was she who was a point ahead. On the fifth shot the gamekeeper evened the score again, but she just beat him to the inner on the sixth and last shot; and so she had won the match.

From the ring of spectators came another murmur, and a small round of applause. Smiling, the attendant gestured around the display behind him, and invited:

"Take your pick, lassie."

It was only then that the moment of triumph hit Cat, and it made her bold. Laughing, she surveyed the shelves with their stock of toys, their bright and tawdry ornaments. In pride of place among the toys was an enormous woolly rabbit, pale blue in colour, one long ear crazily drooping; and out of that moment's boldness, she announced:

"I'll take *that* – the rabbit. For my wee brother."

The attendant thrust the rabbit into her arms, and she grinned in answer to the grin he gave along with it. Because the baby *might* live, after all, and it *might* be a boy, and so why shouldn't she take the chance with this ridiculous thing, this –

"Bloody little tink!" Startled, she swung round to the

voice breaking into the excited rush of her thoughts, and realised that the snarling words had come from the gamekeeper. He was glaring down at her, his thin face suffused with angry colour. But even supposing he *was* feeling bitter over his defeat, that didn't give him the right to call her names, did it? And how did he know, anyway, that she was a traveller?

Shaken, Cat stared back at the man. She didn't look any different, did she, from a hundred girls she had seen that day? Jeans and cotton top – she was dressed exactly as they had been. And her jeans weren't scruffy, either, like the ones worn by some of those other girls. Her face was clean, her hair combed –

"Course she's a tink!" The man was looking over her head, shouting towards some of the spectators who had protested at his outburst. "Look at that bloody dog of hers!"

Cat looked, as everyone else had begun to look at Shuffler standing at full stretch of the cord that tied him to the post beside the shooting gallery. Shuffler had sensed she was in trouble. He was snarling, the choke chain pulling tight around his neck as he tried to reach her. And in a setting like that, of course, with all those pure-bred dogs around, he was so obviously a cross-bred . . . Knowledgeably from the crowd, a voice remarked:

"Aye, a lurcher."

"What did I tell you?" The gamekeeper waved his arms, inviting the crowd to agree with him. "That's a tink dog, if ever there was one – the kind they always use. And so she must be one o' them, the crowd that's camped west of the town, that filthy lot! So what's she doin' here, eh, stickin' her nose in among decent folk?"

He was roaring now – he had to roar against the noise

that had broken out in the crowd. And the noise, Cat realised, was all hostile to her. With difficulty she controlled her shaking fingers enough to untie Shuffler from his post, and pushed her way free of the crowd. Voices followed her as she pushed, jeering voices, threatening voices, and among them she heard again a reference to "that filthy lot west of the town." But who were they, those travellers who had raised such resentment that the crowd which had applauded her shooting should turn so violently against her as soon as they thought she was one of them?

Determinedly, once she was clear of the Game Fair, she strode towards the town, and followed the road that ran westwards from its centre. On the outskirts of the western suburbs lay a stockyard and a huddle of cattle sheds, with field and woodland beyond. But between the stockyard and the first of the fields there was a stretch of waste ground, and it was there that she found the camp.

She stood and stared at it, dismay overtaking her at the squalid sight it presented, with trucks and trailers tilted at awkward angles on the uneven ground, piles of rusty scrap iron beside some of the trailers, litter scattered broadcast, and mud-streaked children tumbling about among the rubbish.

A woman's face peered at her from one of the trailers, and her dismay deepened as she realised that the camp had no source of water except the river running almost quarter of a mile from it. So how could any of the women there cook, or wash, without breaking their backs humping every drop of water that was needed? As for keeping themselves and their bairns clean . . .

Her gaze travelled to a group of men sitting on upturned boxes. The men were drinking beer out of cans, and from the noise they were making, it seemed to her that they had already drunk more than enough. Two of the men rose and left the group as she watched, and came walking towards her; but neither of them, she noticed with surprise, was a traveller, and neither of them showed any sign of the drunkenness in the group they had just left.

The shorter of the two men was dressed in a neat business suit. The taller man was a lot more casually dressed, but she could see a big gold earring glinting in one of his ears; and that was certainly not the mark of a traveller man. It was this earringed man who dominated the conversation as the two of them walked, his voice loud and boastful. The talk continued as they drew to a halt quite close to where she stood, and it was then that she heard the boastful one declare:

"But you'll see, Ballantyne, the Council will have to do something about it now. All that stuff in the newspapers, you see, it was bad publicity for them. And that's just what we need to force their hand on it."

"You're wrong." The man in the business suit shook his head. "I've told you before how wrong you are. And worse than that, Reevel, every time you do something like this you set *my* work back. But you'll find out yet that I'm as stubborn as you are."

The man called "Reevel" laughed. The other man turned abruptly from him to walk in the direction of the stockyard; and with a tug of Shuffler's lead, Cat ran after him. "Ballantyne" – that was what the Reevel man had called him – and she *thought* she had recognised his face!

"Dr Ballantyne! Hey, wait!" He turned at her call, then halted; and for a moment, as she and Shuffler came up to him, she was awkwardly afraid that she had made a

130

mistake. But, no, he was the Dr Ballantyne who had sorted out, years ago, the trouble she and Rhona had run into at school; and shyly she reminded him of that before she ventured to ask:

"What's it all about, the state of the camp back there? I nearly got lynched this afternoon at the Game Fair when folk thought I was one of that lot."

"Did you, indeed?" Dr Ballantyne shot her a grim, unsurprised look, then nodded towards the stockyard. "My car's parked along there. Walk with me, and I'll tell you the score." Cat fell into step with him, and after a moment, he continued:

"Those people back there – they came expecting to find a site they'd used for years – one that's even further west of the town; a nice site, close to the river and well hidden from the road. But that's gone now. There's a luxury hotel built on it, and the waste ground was the only other site they could find. But that's an old story by this time – eh?"

"Aye." Cat nodded, with visions of one vanished camp site another another slipping through her mind – all of them once traditional stopping-places for travellers, all of them now overtaken by the kind of circumstance Dr Ballantyne had mentioned. "There's many a place," she offered, "where we used to stop and that's gone from us now. And then, when we did find some new place, like as not the polis would come along and chase us out of it."

"They can't do that now," Dr Ballantyne told her sharply. "Not since folk like me managed to get the Government to agree to an official policy of 'no-harassment.' In plain terms, a policy that forbade any bullying of travellers, any attempt to move them on whenever the local police decided it was time to get rid of them."

Like Sergeant McKendrick! Cat felt a shiver of remembrance for the threatening figure that had appeared on the day of the cuckoo snow, and that had menaced them again after the potato harvest on Jack Brownlee's farm. Sergeant McKendrick, she thought grimly, wouldn't have taken at all kindly to a policy of no-harassment!

"And that wasn't the end of it, either." Dr Ballantyne had continued speaking over her thought. "Because something had to be done to replace the loss of those traditional sites; something that took account of other changes in traveller life – like the way some of the men have had to turn to dealing in scrap, for instance, now that farming's so mechanised that there's not the same call for their labour. And so the next step was for Government to order local authorities to provide sites for travellers who *could* make a living in their area, either just passing through or for the long-term stays when the children have to do their schooling; properly serviced sites, too, with water laid on, and refuse collection, and storage space for stuff that's being dealt in – "

"And rent to pay?" Dr Ballantyne had become so carried away with what he was saying that Cat had to be quick at slipping in her question; but just as quickly, he agreed:

"Yes, yes. All the travellers who've been consulted over this have agreed right away that it was only fair they should pay the kind of rent that would cover all the services. But the trouble is, you see, that the authorities have given us more talk than action over providing the sites; and that's where Reevel – Reevel Faw, the man you saw me talking to – that's where he comes in."

"There was something about that one," Cat remarked. "He looked like a gypsy to me."

"That's just what he is." They had reached Dr Ballantyne's car by this time, and he was unlocking the door as he answered Cat. "And he's here because he's trying to make himself a power among Scottish travellers the way he's managed to do that with his own gypsy folk, in England – using the same tactics on their behalf as he's already used for the so-called benefit of those English gypsies."

So-called. Cat pondered the word, wondering at the implications in it. Suspicion in her voice, she asked, "What about these tactics, then? What are they?"

"Bad ones; bad in every way. What he does, you see, is to collect the very worst he can find among travelling folk – the drunks, the layabouts, the nasty characters, all the kind of scum you'll find among any group of people – and dump them down among some decent travellers who've been forced to camp on waste ground near a town. Then the trouble starts, with this scum invading the town, getting fighting-drunk, smashing the place up and generally making a disgusting nuisance of themselves. That brings in the newspapers – sometimes even the TV cameras. And what should they find but our friend Reevel, all ready to give interviews about the bad deal travellers are getting, and how can they be blamed for letting off steam about it?"

"But wait a minute!" In surprise and growing anger, Cat broke in to Dr Ballantyne's next words. "Travellers – ordinary travellers – aren't like that bunch of no-goods. And people know they're not."

"Aw, come on, Cat! Use your head! I shouldn't have to tell you that 'people' don't know anything about travellers – except that they've always come and gone so quietly that nobody ever noticed them before. Before Reevel started his tricks, that is. But once that's happened, those same people do notice them in a way that makes them think of travellers as a threat to life and limb – which makes them willing to consider anything that'll stop the mayhem. So what does Reevel do then? Why, he whistles off his shock troops, and offers himself to the local Council as a negotiator for the ones that are left – the quiet, decent travellers that nobody has ever previously given a thought to. And that way, you see, he hopes to get them the site they're entitled to."

"But not before he's blackened their name!" Cat exclaimed. "And that's a dirty trick, a real rotten thing to do."

Dr Ballantyne sighed. "Try telling that to Reevel. He not only wants to be a big shot, he belongs to the school of thought that believes the end justifies the means. But listen, Cat. Travellers have been misrepresented before, and they will be again. It's part of the penalty that you and your kind pay for your way of life. So don't let what you've seen today trouble you too much – eh?" An encouraging hand touched Cat's shoulder. The face looking down at her began to smile.

"Just keep in mind, instead, that Reevel's not the only pebble on the beach – far from it, because there's still my organisation pushing away at all the local authorities, prodding them all the time to get on with providing those sites they're supposed to provide. Keep in mind, too, that we've already had some success – and that *without* doing any damage to the travellers themselves. And we'll have more yet, believe me. So the future maybe isn't as dark as you thought it was."

The eyes looking down at her were kind, not the eyes of a man who told lies. That, Cat remembered, was what she had thought on the day he had argued with Old Nan.

"I believe you," she said. "But you don't have to bother about me – honest, you don't. Because I'm not bothered about the future, you see. I can handle it."

"I don't doubt that!" Dr Ballantyne laughed a little over the words, and slid behind the wheel of his car. With a hand out to close the door, he nodded towards the blue rabbit she held tucked under one arm, and asked; "That monstrosity – tell me, how did you come by it?"

"I won it." Puzzled, and somewhat defensive too, now, Cat renewed her clutch on the rabbit. "I won it shooting at the Game Fair."

"Oh? There's quite a few sporting types usually go in for that sort of thing. You must have shot well."

"Well enough!" With pride rising in her at remembrance of the shooting match, Cat could not resist adding, "Against a gamie, too. A man that's a shooter to trade."

"I'm not surprised. You have the look of a winner about you – a determined look." Dr Ballantyne was smiling again as he spoke, and the smile inspired Cat to another burst of confidence.

"I still have your card," she said. "The one you gave my Nan, years ago."

"Use it, then. Whenever you think you need help, give me a shout." His smile became a grin, a broadly-admiring sort of grin that made her blush. "But remember what I said. You're a natural to come out on top of any situation you tackle!"

He closed the car door, waved, and was away. Cat stood for a moment staring after the departing car. It was strange, she thought, that a man like him – well-educated and all that – should be so concerned about travellers; strange in a nice sort of way. No wonder she'd been tempted to let her tongue run away with her! But still, it had been a mistake to mention that card. She shouldn't have done that, shouldn't have allowed her vision of Rhona to surface out of the past . . .

Uneasily she pushed this regret away from her and set off towards the camp with her thoughts firmly concentrated, instead, on the pleasure her parents would show when she presented the toy for the new baby.

10

"I want to speak to you," Ilsa told Cat. "And what I have to say has to be kept secret between the two of us."

Ilsa still had the air of serenity that had marked the whole of her pregnancy; but she was very near her time now, and Cat had the feeling she was going to talk about the baby. Uneasily she glanced at the Game Fair prize, the blue rabbit, and wished once again that she had never brought the thing back with her.

Not that her mother hadn't been delighted with it, of course, just as she'd hoped would happen. But gradually, in her own imagination, it had become a sinister thing, a reminder of all the things that could go wrong with the birth, so that there might be no baby, after all, to laugh at such a ridiculous toy. Nervously she faced again to her mother; and, calm as ever, Ilsa said what she had to say, bearing down all interruptions, refusing to be put off by the growing horror in the eyes fixed on her own.

"I won't! I won't!" Cat finally had her chance to protest, and she seized it with all the energy at her command. "I *can't*, Mammy. I couldn't even try. And you've no right to ask me."

"I'm not asking. I'm telling you. And you will do it. Because that's the only way to save this bairn."

"You're off your head! You're clean daft!" Cat wrung her hands in agitation. "It'll be the other way round, Mammy. And if it dies, it'll be *my* fault!"

"Cat!" Ilsa caught hold of the squirming hands and forced Cat's gaze to meet her own. "I've given you my reasons, and they're all good ones. But now I'll give you the best one of all; the one that'll tell you why it *has* to be the way I said."

Quietly, Ilsa went on speaking, and there was such intensity in the quiet tone that Cat could not help but listen. In the eyes that held her own there was such a strange glow of conviction that she could not help being affected by it. Her common-sense reeled, and began to surrender. Yet still, in the end, she tried to make her surrender a conditional one.

"You'll have to help me, Mammy – show me, teach me what to do."

Her mother nodded. "I will, Cat. I'll teach you beforehand, and I'll help you every step of the way."

"And my Daddy – what am I goin' to tell him? *He'll* never agree, even though I do."

"You won't tell your Daddy, and neither will I, until it's too late for him to do anything about it."

"It won't ever be too late so far as he's concerned. He'll still pack you into the car and rush you off to the hospital."

Ilsa smiled. "Ah, but Cat! You can think of ways to deal with that, can you not?"

And she could too, Cat realised. There was one very simple way, in fact, that had sprung immediately to her mind. And, she realised also, her mother already knew she had thought of it. Her mother, as so often had happened before, had read her thoughts before she could voice them even to herself! On impulse, she exclaimed:

"If you'd lived in olden times, Mammy, they'd have burned you for a witch!"

"Very likely." Ilsa nodded a smiling agreement, then slyly added, "Although maybe, seeing you're another o' the same kind, they'd have burned you along wi' me."

She smiled again, and this time, Cat also found herself smiling. Because of what? she wondered. It was done now. She was committed to a course of action, even although the thought of it still terrified her. And yet – Her mother's eyes were as intent as ever. Her mother's grasp on her hands had continued firm. And through that grasp, that look, there was a feeling flowing, a sense of secret, female kinship that flattered at the same time as it reassured her. Instinctively she returned the pressure of her mother's hands, and told her:

"Just give me good warning, Mammy, and I promise I'll stand by you the best I can."

It was two days later that Ilsa gave Cat the needed warning – a mere look over the breakfast tea, but that was enough. Cat rose, her prepared excuse to stay with her mother that day all ready on her tongue; and the moment her father had set off to his day's work at the pearling, she and Ilsa swung into action.

Plastic to cover the couch that would be Ilsa's bed, a supply of clean drawsheets to place over the plastic, boiling water to sterilize the strong linen thread that would tie the baby's cord, and the scissors that would cut the cord, a warm-lined box for the baby itself, a bucket for swabs – under her breath Cat counted off all the items they would need.

Her hands shook as she worked, not because it was cold in the trailer, but because she was scared. Freely she made the admission to herself, and tried to counter it with the knowledge that she had already seen birth many times

139

before then – lambs, foals, calves, she had seen all these being born. And twice she had sat by while Sheba was having a litter of pups.

But a dog was a dog, a pup was a pup, and it was a human baby and her own Mammy she would have to deal with. That was the big difference. That was why she couldn't help being scared. And so why couldn't it have been Old Nan who was there instead of her? Why couldn't it have been anybody except herself – even somebody from the hospital, in spite of the fact that her mother was so determined not to have the baby there?

"Y'all right, lassie?" Ilsa's voice, anxiously enquiring, made her suddenly ashamed of her preoccupation with self.

"I'm fine, Mammy, just fine." As cheerfully as she could, Cat threw the answer back over her shoulder, and turned to ask, "How often are you getting the pains now?"

"Every twenty minutes." Her mother was standing bent over with one hand pressing into the small of her back, the other clutching the bulge of her belly. Her face was white, and she spoke with a gasp in her voice.

"Will you manage to get yourself ready?"

"Aye, fine that. And while I'm busy about it, you can see to the car."

Cat stepped outside the trailer, shivering at the touch of the late September air on her face. Shuffler bounded up to her as she walked towards the car. Shuffler was on his own now, with Sheba off to the pearling with her father, and he wasn't much liking that. She raised the bonnet of the car, reached for the distributor cap, and unclipped it. Shuffler watched her all the time she worked inside the car, his head on one side, ears cocked in question.

When she had finished, she closed the bonnet and bent over him, her hands busy at his neck. Patiently he accepted her actions, with no more than a puzzled shake of the head at the result, and went back to his resting place on a pile of sacks under the trailer. Cat went inside to scrub her hands clean of the grease the car had left on them, and to check on her mother.

Ilsa was feeling the urge to walk about between pains, and there was now only a fifteen minute interval between one pain and the next. Cat steadied her with an arm as they walked together up and down the narrow confines of the trailer; and they talked as they walked, disjointedly, in sentences that broke off sometimes, or sometimes trailed into silence. The blue rabbit watched them from the shelf where Ilsa had placed it, and Cat tried her hardest not to read meaning into the meaningless, glassy gaze.

The pains began to be more frequent and to last longer. Ilsa declared herself ready to lie down; and almost immediately after this, Cat saw the flow of blood and mucus that came from her to spread redly over the bedsheet. She panicked, standing stock-still, with one hand flying to her open, exclaiming mouth; but quickly, Ilsa reassured her:

"It's all right, it's only what they call a 'show'. But get your swabs. That's what they're there for."

Cat rushed to obey, her mother's very calmness shaming her into action, and when the stained sheet had been replaced by another, Ilsa told her:

"Now, remember, Cat, the next thing to expect is the breaking of the waters – the water lying around the baby. You'll see it come from me, just the same way as the show. But that's nothing to be frightened of, either, because all it'll mean is that I'll very likely be ready to go into the second stage of the labour."

"And that's when the baby'll start on its way out?"

"Too true, lassie! But if you do everything the way I've told you – " Ilsa paused to smile up at Cat. " – between us, we'll see it safely born."

If my Daddy doesn't get here first. It was getting late in the afternoon by then, the short September day dying, and the thought passing through Cat's mind at that moment was one that kept recurring with each fresh pain that Ilsa experienced. Because the labour was definitely speeding up now, she realised; and so it could not be very much longer before those ever-more-frequent pains became the overwhelmingly powerful ones that her mother had warned would mark the end of its first stage. And that would produce more than the groans coming from her now!

Ilsa leaned forward, knees drawn up, hands clutching her knees. As the gathering contraction took on force, her breath came out in a series of gasps and groans. The sound that came from her at the climax of pain was like a low, whining scream. The pain began to ebb. She let her shoulders slump back on to the pillows Cat had piled behind her. Eyes closed, she panted:

"Not long – now – Cat. A few more – strong ones like that and – we'll be there."

Her final words were overlaid by sounds from outside the trailer – greeting noises between Shuffler and Sheba, Jim's voice speaking to both dogs, the clank of a pearling jug being laid against the trailer's outer wall.

Ilsa's eyes flew wide open, but there was no need for her to voice the anxiety in them. Cat was already moving to the door of the trailer, throwing a quick word of reassurance over her shoulder as she went. In the day's dying light she saw her father turn to her, a question ready on his lips; and sharply she cut into his words:

"It's happening, Daddy. The baby's on its way."

"Right!" The gear her father had been holding dropped from his hands. "I'll get the car started, and we'll have her in hospital in no time."

"No, Daddy. She's not goin' into hospital." Cat stood determinedly in the way of her father's movement towards the car. "She'll have it here, and I'll birth it for her."

"Eh?" Jim stared, his jaw dropping in astonishment, and Cat hurried on:

"Because it's the way she wants it to be, Daddy. She's dead set on that. But I know what to do. She told me. She told me everything, right down to the business of the afterbirth, and cutting the baby's cord. And so it's goin' to be all right – really it is."

"You want your head looked at, girl, and so does she!" Jim had his breath back now, and angrily he went on, "So stand clear and let me get that car. I'm takin' her to the hospital, whether she likes it or not."

"Daddy, listen." Still obstinately blocking his way and clinging to his jacket sleeve when he tried to pass her, Cat persisted with her argument. "Please, Daddy, listen and try to understand. She's feared of hospitals. And she's got reason to be. Women that go there to have babies, she says, get treated like lumps of meat – not like people. It's all machines and gadgets and bright lights about you, instead of like it should be, with just folk talkin' kind and quiet to you. And the midwives, if you cry out with the pain, they just dope you or else they tell you you're a coward and they've seen far worse births in their time.

And the doctors bring their students along and they all poke around inside you, a lot of men with hard fingers poking away and hurting you, and it's like being raped but they don't think like that, they never think that's how it feels to you – "

She was babbling now and she knew it – and what was she doing anyway using words like "raped" in front of her Daddy? But she didn't care, he would have to listen because somehow she had to convince him as Mammy had convinced her . . .

" – and it's bad enough for other women but it's worse for Mammy because she's a traveller and everybody looks down on her for being a traveller and the other women don't talk to her and what has she got at the end of it? Nothing, nothing she's got nothing – just a dead baby and that's worse than nothing, and I won't – "

"Let go!" With an anger she had never seen in him before, her father interrupted and broke her hold so forcefully that she was sent spinning from him. "That's *my* bairn that's being born – *my* son. And it'll be in hospital where he'll have the proper care he should have. And his Mammy too."

"But you can't take her there!" Cat shrieked the words after him as he strode to the car. "You can't, because the car's no use to you. I've taken the rotor arm out of it."

"You've *what*?" Jim swung back to her. In the gathering dusk, his face was thunderous.

"I've taken the rotor arm out of it." Cat backed from him, afraid of his anger, but still determined to carry through what she had started. "But I don't have it on me, Daddy, so it's not use comin' nearer. And it's not hidden anywhere, either, but it's still where you'll never get it."

She pointed to Shuffler, lying beside Sheba, the small

144

canvas bag into which she had put the rotor arm still strung around his neck, its pale colour standing out clearly against the black of his hide. Jim's gaze flew to the bag. Imperiously he called:

"Here, Shuffler, here!"

Shuffler rose and began obediently to trot towards him.

"Stay!" Cat shouted; and obediently again, Shuffler halted and held his position. Jim began to walk towards him, a hand outstretched in readiness to take the bag from around his neck. Cat shouted again, "Stand off, Shuffler. Stand off!"

Shuffler's upper lip lifted in a snarl. He back away from Jim, warily, snarling all the time, Jim came to a halt. He looked from the dog showing its teeth in menace, to the tense and defiant form of the girl.

"And to think it was me," he said bitterly, "that showed you how to train that dog."

"That's right." Breathlessly Cat agreed. "So you know the score now, Daddy. He'll stand off from you till I tell him different. Because he's *my* dog, and so it's *my* voice that's needed to break that order. I'm sorry, Daddy, but – "

"Listen!" Her father held up a hand in sudden warning, and it was only then that she heard the sound that had wrenched his attention from her – Ilsa's voice starting up a cry from inside the trailer. And the sound was growing, growing! It was rising in pitch and volume until it was half-shriek, half-shout. And wholly terrible!

"Oh, my God, oh *do* something, Cat!" With his hands to his ears to shut out the reality of the sound, Jim called out a plea that jerked Cat from her frozen stance of horror at the sound. And on winged feet, then, she went speeding back to her mother.

145

11

It was much dimmer inside the trailer than it had been outside. Cat had to light the butane gas lamp before she could see Ilsa's face, still contorted with the agony that had forced the cry from her. She bent over the bed, her insides quivering yet from the impact it had made on her, and forced her voice to come out as naturally as possible.

"How are you, Mammy?"

"Managing. I'm – managing. And there can't be – more than – another one like that – still – to come." Ilsa was gasping as she spoke. "But – your Daddy? Did you tell him?"

"I told him."

"That's a good lassie."

Cat moved to draw the curtains against the anguished face of her father staring in through the window. She washed her hands of the traces the lamp had left on them, and when she turned back to the bed again, Ilsa was getting ready for the next pain.

Her knees were once more drawn up. The knuckles of the hands grasped around them were white with tension. She began to pant, then to moan. Her moans grew louder, till she was once more making the terrifying sound that had brought Cat rushing back into the trailer.

Hands clenched, nails biting into her palms, Cat shuddered back from the sound; and then, in an agony of sympathy for her mother, she was bending over the bed, clutching Ilsa's writhing hands tight in her own, weeping, crying out to her in a wordless love that begged to share the pain. Ilsa's body fused with her own. For a moment, they were poised together on the same high point of endurance.

The moment receded with the fading of the pain. Sound died. The locked hands loosened. From Ilsa now came only whimpers that trailed away and faded to nothing. Her taut body relaxed. She lay back on the pillows, the lines of her face slackening, her eyes closed. Wearily, as Cat bathed sweat from her brow, she whispered:

"That's it. I've had enough babies by this time to know. That pain was the last of the strong ones."

Cat drew back from her, relief at the words fighting fear of what was coming next. Shakily, she answered:

"Rest then, while you can, Mammy. And here – " With gentle movements she drew over Ilsa the blanket that would keep her warm while she waited for the second stage of the labour to begin. "Keep this over you."

"In a minute, hen." Ilsa put the blanket aside and began struggling to sit up. "You'll have to change the sheet first."

The fear in Cat's mind broke from her in a gasp as she saw that the sheet beneath her mother was wet, but Ilsa was ready for this reaction.

"Now, don't fret," she soothed. "It's nothing more than the waters breaking – just like I warned you would happen."

Cat nodded, not trusting herself to speak, at first; but once she had changed the wet sheet for a dry one, she was once more in command of herself.

"And what's to come now," her mother told her then,

"the second stage of the labour, Cat – that'll be hard work for me. But hard work is all it'll be. So you'll have no need to fret over that either – eh?"

"None at all, Mammy." As comfortingly as she could, Cat agreed, and went on with the one further job that had to be done – that of knotting a strip of towelling to the wooden framework of the couch so that Ilsa would have something to pull on as a counter to the bearing-down pains of the second stage.

There was no sound, after that, in the trailer, nothing except her own and her mother's breathing and the slight hissing noise of the gas lamp – until suddenly, Ilsa exclaimed:

"The baby – it's on the way now!" Her face became tense. Her breathing hung suspended on a long intake of air. "I – Oh, Cat, I want to bear down, to push, to push . . . "

Cat was on her feet in the instant, and thrusting the free end of the towelling strip into her mother's hands. "Here, Mammy! Here!"

Ilsa's reaching fingers curled around the material, clawing a way up it till her arms were stretched out well above her shoulders and she was pulling frantically against the knot Cat had tied.

"Good, good!" Cat encouraged her. "You'll be able to bear down real hard now, Mammy."

Ilsa's only answer to this was a grunt, succeeded by a long, slow exhalation of breath as the bearing-down pain came gradually to its end. Cat wiped the sweat from her mother's brow, and then moved to the foot of the bed wondering how many more of such pains were still to come. *Because it wasn't as if Mammy was young any more – not young like herself and Rhona. And if she* didn't have enough strength left now to keep pushing really hard . . .

"That's it! Come on, now, come on!" *What did happen anyway, if a mother wasn't strong enough to help her baby out?* "Push, Mammy! Keep pushing!" *Would the baby just stick there, and suffocate?* "Oh, you're doin' real good, Mammy! Just keep it up, keep it up!"

With each successive bearing-down pain after that first one, Cat's voice rang out in encouragement of her mother's efforts, and Cat's mind whirled in an ever-thickening fog of bewilderment and fear of approaching disaster. Because those same efforts *weren't* strong enough. Her mother was tiring, beginning to pant now, instead of drawing in the deep breath needed for each push. And she did so want this baby!

Through the fog in Cat's mind, piercing it like a ray of light, came the fleeting memory of a sunlit clearing in a pinewood and the figure of her mother dancing there, dancing out her grief for all the dead babies. The odd protectiveness she had felt for her mother that day welled up in her again, so suddenly, so strongly, that there was no longer room for fear in her mind, no longer room for anything but determination that *this* baby, at least, would be born alive. She leaned over her mother as the next bearing-down pain gathered way, and shouted at her, shouted boldly and exultantly the lie that had sprung to her mind.

"I can see the head, Mammy! I can see the head!"

Ilsa's exhausted face flickered into fresh life. Her grip on the towelling tightened convulsively. Cat's voice filled the trailer again, a demanding voice this time, a harsh and bullying one.

"So push now, damn you! If you want this baby – push!"

Ilsa closed her eyes, drew in her breath, and pushed, with every muscle of her abdomen and diaphragm straining to its utmost. And to Cat's amazement and delight, the push *did* give her a sight of the baby's head, the dark-haired crown of it just beginning to show, wet and smooth, between her mother's thighs.

"That's a good Mammy!" Her voice gentle now, and a little shaky from the emotional shock of the moment, Cat continued her encouragement. "Just one more push now. Just one. That's all that's needed."

Ilsa began gathering her strength for the effort, sucking air deep into her lungs, gritting her teeth in concentration. And once again, as she pushed, power surged into her muscles. There was a yielding and stretching of the tissues surrounding the first small appearance of the head, a further and further stretching until they had given to their utmost, and the entire crown of the head was visible.

"Short breaths now, Mammy!" Cat spoke very quickly, urgently remembering how her mother had warned that any futher pushing at this stage might tear those stretched tissues. "Only short breaths now, and you'll have the head out, no bother. And no damage to yourself, either."

Ilsa's breathing altered, became quick and shallow. The baby's head began sliding into the open. It came slowly, tilting backward as it came, so that Cat's view of its crown was followed by her first sight of a forehead, a brow, a nose, a mouth, a chin, a whole and perfect human face gradually revealing itself – *like a flower unfolding!* With awe and wonder as the words of the comparison shot through her mind, Cat held her hands cupped to receive that backward-tilting head.

It rested there, between her palms. She waited, all

conscious thought suspended, all feeling concentrated on that small, warm weight within the cup of her hands. Ilsa drew more of her quick, shallow breaths and, one after the other, the baby's shoulders slid smoothly into the open. With infinite care, Cat adjusted her hold so that she could extend her support of the baby with fingertips under its armpits. The entire length of its body slid free; and from the pursed-up mouth in the small, damp face came a sound that started out as a feeble mewing and grew to a lusty cry.

Ilsa began trying to raise herself, eyes straining for a sight of the baby. But Cat was already lifting it towards her, both arms cradling its slipperiness, the long length of cord that bound it still to Ilsa's body, redly trailing. Ilsa lay back, taking the baby with her. Its head moved, blindly nuzzling her breast. It cried again, and she smiled. There were tears rolling down her face, but still she smiled a smile of such utter happiness that Cat also found herself in the peculiar situation of smiling – laughing, even – at the same time as she, too, wept. Ilsa said weakly:

"Your Daddy – "

Cat nodded, and went to the window. She opened it a crack, and looked out to the dark figure hunched against the trailer's outer wall. In the ray of light from the window she saw the grim lines into which her father's face had set, the staring anxiety in his eyes; and quickly she told him:

"They're both all right, Daddy. And it's a wee laddie you have now."

He gaped, the grim face gone suddenly stupid with relief, and stammered, "Can I – Can I see them?"

"Not till everything's properly over." Firmly she

closed the window and turned back to her mother with her mind now full of all the other things that had to be done. The linen thread to tie the baby's cord, scissors to cut the cord, a dressing to put over the stump of it – carefully she went over the procedure her mother had taught her; and with Ilsa encouraging her at every step, she carried it through without a hitch. Quietly then, Ilsa told her:

"I'm proud of you, Cat." And for the first time that day, it occurred to Cat herself to be proud of her efforts.

Blushing, she wrapped the baby warmly and placed it in the box made ready for it before she began to attend again to her mother – this time to make sure that the afterbirth was properly expelled. It was coming away intact, she found, and – thank God! – there was no bleeding. Her Mammy was safe! Now it really *was* all over, and her Mammy was safe from this last of the dangers she had faced!

With relief making her feel almost lightheaded, Cat cleared up at the end of the process, then made Ilsa once more clean and comfortable; and it was only after she had conscientiously dealt with all this that she finally ventured the question she had meanwhile been bursting to ask – the same question that had hovered in her mind ever since her mother had first told her if would be up to her to birth the baby.

"Mammy – " She spoke with its shawl-wrapped form all ready to be returned to her mother. "Remember what you said to me about the gift – that it was the gift that told you I would be the one to birth the bairn?" She hesitated, rocking the baby in her arms to soothe the little cries it had begun to make. "I was wondering – I mean, what was it like for you then? What did you actually *see?*"

"I saw you, Cat." With that glow of happiness still on her face, Ilsa held Cat's gaze with her own. "I saw you standing just like you're standing now with the bairn, new-born, in your arms. Just for a flash I saw you like that, here in the trailer. And just for the flash, too, I heard the cries he's making now. That was all. But it was enough to tell me what had to be done. Because you have to trust the gift, Cat, even when you feel you don't want to, even when other people think you're being stupid – or even when your own common-sense says that you *are* being stupid. Because it wouldn't be there in you, would it, if you weren't meant to trust it? But now lassie – " Smiling, Ilsa held out her arms for the baby. "It's time to call your Daddy."

Cat lowered the baby into her mother's arms, and went to the door of the trailer. Her father came hurrying at her first call. He brushed past her in the doorway, but she did not see what happened after that. She was tired, suddenly, so tired that all she wanted to do was to sit down somewhere and rest.

She closed the trailer door and sat on the step outside it. Her hands drooped down between her knees, her head leaned back against the door, her eyes closed; but behind her eyes still was the image of the new-born baby lying between his mother's legs, the cord that bound him to her all red and pulsating with their shared life.

That cord! Hadn't it been wonderful to see – her Mammy's life and the baby's life beating together in it! And the moment she had watched the sight of the baby's face revealing itself . . . She smiled, remembering how it had seemed to her that it had been like watching a flower unfolding. Then suddenly she found she was weeping again, tears of exhaustion this time, maybe, or maybe even tears of self-pity for all she had gone through – she didn't really know what the tears were for, except that they had something to do with being married and having babies.

Or maybe they came from *not* being married, and *not* having babies; because here she was within a few months of sixteen and still no nearer to making up her mind about Charlie Drummond than she had been on the day he had saved her from the yobbos at the pool – the day he had told her that he'd marked her down. But it was one thing for Charlie to say that, and quite another thing – wasn't it? – for her to say she *would* marry him. There were such important things still standing in the way of that, even although – for the first time Cat admitted it to herself – even although she knew very well that she did want to marry him.

The dogs had come crowding around her, attention-seeking as always. She fondled them both, rubbed tears off on Shuffler's fur, and spoke forlornly to him.

"I can't put it off much longer, either, making up my mind what to do about Charlie. Not with both of us at the age now where it's high time we were married."

Shuffler whined, and jealously tried to nose Sheba out of his way. She pushed both dogs from her, and tried to concentrate. She had the gift, after all; and the gift had told her she would go back one day to Old Nan's enchanted land, to stand there with Charlie's arm around her. Yet how could that be if she didn't marry him? Eyes closed, fingertips pressed against her eyelids, she began trying to summon up the gift so that she could make it tell her how to deal with the problems that had to be solved before she could agree to marry Charlie.

But the gift didn't work that way, it seemed. The gift

couldn't be forced; so that all she could do in the end was to sit there and yield to the stupor of weariness gradually invading her mind. Her father's voice calling was the sound that roused her again. She rose, faintly surprised to find herself moving so stiffly, wondering from this how long she had sat with her mind blank; and with a last word to the dogs, went back into the trailer. Her father spoke as she came in, looking up from where he sat with one arm around Ilsa and the baby.

"Your Mammy says it's time you had another look at the dressing on the baby's cord, Cat, and then she wants a cup of tea. But here, before you do any of that – " His face one big broad grin of delight, he stretched his free arm towards her. "Come and give your Daddy a cuddle. Come and give us all a cuddle!"

Cat went towards the bed. She knelt beside it and was swept into an embrace, with her father and mother each enclosing an arm around her shoulders, the downy head of the new baby soft as feathers against her cheek; and, it seemed to her then, there was something happened in that embrace. In the feeling that flowed from it, they were no longer four, but simply one – a supremely happy, supremely loving one.

Which was all that really mattered, she told herself; but once she was out of the closeness of the embrace, she was not so sure she had been right in that. And by the time she came to put the kettle on she was thinking yet again about Charlie and the problems that had to be solved before she could marry him.

12

The baby was named James, of course, after his father; and, for short, he was "Jamie." Cat weighed him in at a lively eight pounds on the spring balance that she and her father used for weighing salmon, and they all made plans for showing him off as soon as possible to the others of their wide family circle.

The pearling season was in its last days, after all, and so there was nothing there to stop them heading for the farmlands of Perthshire where those others would already have gathered to work at the potato harvest. Most conveniently, too, it was in the town of Perth itself that they would be able to sell the results of their summer's work to the jeweller who specialised in river pearls. And with the money they got for their pearls, Jim declared, he would buy a really good car and trailer to replace the outfit they had.

"Because that's the only way," he added fondly, "to do justice to our wee lordship here. Now isn't that so?"

Certainly it was, both Cat and her mother agreed in the same fond tones, their eyes worshipping the pink, contented baby nursing at Ilsa's breast.

"But where will you get this car and trailer?" Practical as ever, Cat tried then to pin her father down on the details of the plan; and was briefly embarrassed when he told her:

"Through Daddler Drummond, of course. It's in Perth

he has his scrapyard, remember. And scrappies like him can always put a fellow in the way of a bargain. Besides – " Jim paused to shoot her a look that deepened her embarrassment. "That'll give you a chance to see Charlie again – eh?"

Cat made no answer to this, and pretended not to notice the look that passed between him and her mother. They had no business, she thought rebelliously, to take it for granted that she would marry Charlie – just because *he* had announced it that way. She had a will of her own, hadn't she? Well, *hadn't* she?

"Cat – " Reluctantly she turned her head to the sound of her mother's voice. "Charlie's a good lad," her mother went on. "And he doesn't mind any longer about you doing the kind of work your daddy does. So there's no drawback there, is there?"

"No, Mammy. No drawback." Curtly Cat answered, then rose to put the dinner on the stove. And standing there with her back to her parents and her expression hidden from them, she thought again of all the other drawbacks there were to her marrying Charlie.

The jeweller in Perth was delighted with their pearls – especially the two that were pear-shaped and so well-matched that they would make a splendid pair of pendant earrings.

"And handsomely we've been paid for them!"

Politely, as they prepared to leave the plush and glass interior of the jewellery store, Jim expressed his satisfaction with the bargain struck over these and their other pearls; and with his newly-acquired wad of money safely stowed away in an inside pocket, he and Cat hurried out to the Drummond scrapyard.

Daddler was there, his breath smelling, as usual, of whisky. And Charlie was there, head cocked to one side to listen intently as he tuned the engine of a small and sporty-looking car. Cat left her father to talk to Daddler, and moved to watch Charlie as he worked.

"Great wee car!" Shouting over the noise of the engine as she caught his eye, he reached into the car to switch off the ignition. "Triumph Vitesse. Go like a bird when I've finished with it. And vintage cars like this fetch a real good price."

"Very likely." In the silence that followed the cutting-off of the engine noise, Cat's answer sounded even curter than she had intended; and Charlie grinned to hear it.

"You don't like cars."

"It's different, travelling by car, from the way we used to travel."

The exchange was nothing more than one flat statement following another. But behind Cat's words there was a sudden sick wave of longing for the childhood days of trudging behind the pony cart, when every yard of the road created its own small adventure of colour and taste and smell, when she could stop to cup water in her hands from a torrent rushing cold and clear over a rockface, or be the first to spot the primroses coming into bloom, or stand and guess which way the circling lark would run when it finally touched the ground in its descent towards the hidden nest, or linger long enough to pick a cupful of wild raspberries while she laughed at Shuffler's attempts to lip his own share of berries off the bush . . .

Slowly she came back to herself to find that Charlie was telling her that he had finished with the scrap business now; that he had taken instead to dealing in fast cars like the Vitesse; and come the summer, of course,

158

when they were all on the road again, he was looking forward to other good buys like this one. And how had *she* been doing, this past two months?

She told him about the pearling and the success they'd had selling their catch, and about the new baby – although she didn't say, of course, that it was she who had birthed Jamie, because that was something she could not talk about except to a woman, or another girl. And had he heard anything about Rhona's new baby?

Rhona's baby was fine, he told her – a wee girl with hair as red as its mammy's – and he would give her directions to the farm where she and Alec were working at the tattie harvest. Then, later on, they would all have a great time to themselves, because all the traveller parents working on the nearby farms had got together to hire a hall in the town that night, for the benefit of their young folks. There was to be a disco, and he would take her to it; afterwards they would talk, and get things settled –

"Get things settled?" Interrupting, she caught him up on the words. "What things?"

"*You* know." Charlie glanced away from her, glanced back again, and smiled – all with an awkwardness that was in great contrast to his former ease of manner. "About us. You and me. Getting married, and all that."

"How can we talk about getting married when you've never asked me to marry you?" The question, it seemed to Cat, had popped out of her mouth without her having had any intention of asking it; and Charlie, she saw, was as much struck by surprise to hear it as she had been herself.

"But I told you, didn't I?" He was staring at her, face creased with bewilderment. "I told you I'd marked you down."

"That's not the same as asking me to marry you. And even if it was, I – well – " Cat faltered to a stop, and shrank back from the growing annoyance in Charlie's look.

"Well?" he challenged; and then, when she continued silent, "All right, then, I'll say it now. Will you marry me – there, is that good enough for you?"

"I – " Cat looked away from him, licking lips that had gone suddenly dry. "I'll have to think about it."

"You've already told me that – two months ago. And two months is long enough to think. Besides, what *is* there to think about, for God's sake?"

Charlie was getting angry. Charlie, the easy-going one of the Drummond family, still had something of his father's temper in him!

"Charlie – " she said, "Charlie – " And now there was pleading in her voice. "D'you remember one day when we were kids, and your Mammy got beaten up, and you were so upset, and I was bothered about you being upset, and we talked about it later and I said I'd never let any man do that to me? And you said how was I going to stop that happening, and I said I didn't know but I'd think of something – d'you remember that, Charlie?"

"Aye, well – " Charlie looked uneasily away from her. "But we were just kids – "

"And d'you remember," she pressed on over the rest of his words, "that day those *shan gadgies* had me trapped in the pool and you saved me, but you were so mad at me for what I'd done that you had your fist drawn back to hit me?"

"But I never! I never did!" Charlie was astonished now, his face full of righteous indignation. "I never touched you, Cat."

"No. But you still thought you had the right to hit me."

They stood staring at one another, she accusingly, he with a look of suddenly-realised guilt. "And that," she said finally, "is how I'll stop it happening to me. I won't marry any man that thinks he has the right to beat me."

"Aw, come on, Cat. You don't have to be like that." Charlie was beginning to recover himself now, trying to pass her words off as lightly as possible. "I've got a bit of a temper sometimes, I know, but I won't take it out on you. Even when I've had drink taken, I promise you, I'll never so much as lay a finger on you."

He was smiling, advancing to her with hands outstretched; but she backed from him with disappointment at his lack of understanding turning swiftly to an anger that made her shout:

"Keep your promises, keep them for somebody that needs them! Because *I* don't! I don't need anything from anybody, Charlie Drummond. And I certainly don't need you to marry me. Because I'm that terrible thing, a split mechanic – remember? I can do anything my Mammy can do, I can do anything my Daddy can do. I can get along anywhere, anytime – even at this sort of thing you're doing now. See!"

Glaring at him, she paused long enough to kick a tyre of the Vitesse. "So stop patting me on the head, will you? Stop thinking I'll come running to you just because you promise never to beat me. Because that's not what I want from you – not, not, *not* what I want!"

She was too breathless by then to continue; and Charlie, it seemed, had nothing to say. They stood in moody silence, not looking at one another. From the corner of her eye, Cat saw her father and Daddler

161

Drummond moving towards them from the far side of the yard, slowly, and talking as they came. She looked at Charlie, feeling his gaze on her; and quietly he asked:

"What do you want, Cat?"

The words she had not known how to order before then came pouring out of her. "Just to be me. Just to be Cat herself. Always, Charlie. And for you to know that. For you to know that I can't be me so long as you think you have that sort of right over me. Because that way, you see, I'd belong to you. I'd belong to you the way a dog belongs, or a horse belongs. And so it wouldn't matter how well you kept your promise – would it? – because that would never give me back myself."

There was a strange look now on Charlie's face, a look that was half-puzzled, half-admiring.

"I'm not sure," he said slowly, "if I know what you mean. But I think I do. And if I'm thinking right, Cat – well, I've been brought up in traveller ways; and so you're asking a lot of me."

"I'm not asking anything you don't expect for yourself."

"All right, then." Charlie drew a deep breath of decision. "I'll go along with you in this, Cat. I've no right to beat you. There!" He smiled at her. "Will that be an end now to your arguments about us getting married?"

"No!" The word came blurting out of Cat, and immediately she was appalled at her own bluntness. Yet still something impelled her on, some desperate desire to have everything in the open at last, however much that might hurt Charlie. "It can't be the end, because – "

"Because what?" Charlie interrupted her, his voice rough with the rage she could see rising in him. "Because of what, eh? Haven't I listened enough to you, haven't I agreed enough? So what d'you want from me now,

162

you – you – " He had begun shouting at her, stepping closer, so close that she could see the spittle flecking his lips. "I'm sick of you and your arguments, sick of you leading me by the nose like I was a bairn, making a fool of me – "

She was backed against the car with the shouting face towering over her. There was no way she could escape it – A hand came over her shoulder, her father's hand, jerking her away from that trapped position.

"That's enough, Charlie. That's *my* lassie you're threatening." Her father's voice came to her, the one sane voice in this morass of misunderstanding with Charlie. His arm came protectively around her, and with a sob of relief, she allowed him to lead her away.

13

There was to be a disco that night, Charlie had said; and the very last thing Cat wanted to do after such a quarrel was to dance at a disco. But in this, of course, she had reckoned without Rhona. Rhona had the whole story out of her within half an hour of their arrival at the farm where the rest of the family were camped; and Rhona was insistent that she should go.

"Because it's the best chance you'll ever have to make it up with Charlie," she pointed out. "And besides, you've worked hard all summer. You're entitled to a wee bit of enjoyment."

Cat looked from her to Alec's mother, Lorna MacDonald, sitting with the red-haired baby Isobel in her arms. Lorna caught the look, and smiled at her over the baby's head.

"Don't forget, Cat," she said, "your mammy's my sister and I'm like her in more than looks, so I know what she'd tell you. Go out and enjoy yourself, lassie, while you can."

"Of course she will!" Rhona declared. "I'll make sure she does. She'll go along with me and Alec and all the others, and we'll have a great time to ourselves. But first, Cat, I'm going to do something about that hair of yours!"

Determinedly, comb in hand, she advanced on Cat; and gradually, as the mirror reflected her changed appearance, Cat felt a weakening of her resistance to the idea of going to the disco. She would be with a whole mob of friends, after all, she reminded herself. And that in itself, would be a change. What was more, there was not only Jamie's birth to celebrate. There was also the reward of the long stint at the pearling. And besides, there was no law that said she had to choose this night to have things out with Charlie . . .

The hall where the disco was being held was on the outskirts of the town. Music blasted from it through the open doorway, and the pavement outside was crowded with young travellers debouching from the assortment of transport that had brought them there. Cat grabbed the arm of her cousin, Drew McPhie, Big Andy's eldest son, to steady herself against the crowd; and together they were swept through the doorway.

The noise and movement in the hall engulfed them. Strobe lights shot blue and green and red through the enveloping dimness, flashing, whirling, eerily transmuting the seething movement to a bubbling witch's cauldron of familiar faces slashed with unfamiliar light. The noise surged with a rhythmic beat, persistent, hypnotic, a beat like that of a giant heart, like all the hearts in the hall beating strangely in unison.

Cat found herself on the dance floor, feet, arms, head moving in time to the beat. Her cousin Drew faced her, his movements mirroring her own. They grinned at one another, and Drew shouted through the noise:

"The mammies and the daddies'll be enjoying their-selves by this time too, eh?"

"Aye, round the fire!" Cat shouted back and they both grinned again, knowing what it would be like in the camp now – all the mammies and daddies seated around the fire, drinking, laughing, talking, singing, to celebrate the two new babies; but always, of course, with Ilsa and Lorna keeping an ear cocked for the slightest cry from either of them. And if the babies did cry – why then, that would be just an excuse to bring them out from their respective trailers to be passed around from hand to hand and admired all over again!

Someone caught Cat's arm and whirled her away from Drew – a dark-haired young man with merry dark eyes, and a slow, insolent grin.

"You're Cat – Catriona McPhie." His voice came to her through the din with a lilting sound that touched a chord of memory in her. "You were at Jack Brownlee's four years ago, picking tatties. And before that, at a wee camp north of Perth."

The little camp that had given her the day of the swans – the explosion of white, winged beauty!

"And you're Kevin – Kevin Reid!" The whole memory was clear now. "Joe and Morven's eldest. But you've grown. You were just a laddie the last time we met."

"Four years has made a difference to you too." The merry dark eyes swept boldly over her. "The kind of difference *I* like to see."

"I'm spoken for." Abruptly, thankfully remembering Charlie, Cat placed her announcement like a barrier between herself and the bold, appraising eyes of Kevin Reid; and was thankful again when the end of the dance released her to rejoin Alec and Rhona.

Rhona, she thought, was looking lovely, her red hair gleaming with its own light, her pale cheeks flushed the delicate pink that was her highest colour. And she was in great spirits! So was everyone, Cat realised, ears absorbing the chatter, eyes glancing over all the smiling faces around her. But where was Charlie? His older brothers were there, all three of them, and he had said he would be there. But where was he now?

The music started up again. Rhona's brother, Hugh, pulled her on to the floor. She danced with him, telling herself that the night was young yet. There was plenty of time still, for Charlie to appear. She danced with Drew again, then with Alec. She danced with Drew's brother, Ali, then with Rhona's other brother, Billy. Still no sign of Charlie! Rhona's oldest brother took her on to the floor. A break in the music brought them to a halt beside a couple coming through the open door of the hall. And Charlie was the male half of the couple.

Charlie had one arm around the shoulders of the girl with him, a dark-haired girl with her face turned towards him. He was speaking to the girl, and as he spoke to her, the fingers of his hand on her shoulder reached up to fondle the big gold earring gleaming in the ear almost hidden by her dark hair. . . . *gold earrings to set off my good looks – big earrings* . . .

Moura Reid! The girl was that flirty little bitch Moura Reid! In the second it took for the words to pass through Cat's mind, Moura Reid looked up, and straight at her. A gasp from Moura as she registered the outrage and astonishment on Cat's face, and Charlie's head also came up. His hand dropped away from its hold on Moura's earring. He opened his mouth to speak, but Cat forestalled anything he had to say.

"You!" Her voice thick with anger, she addressed Moura. "What the hell d'you think *you're* doing?"

Moura's dark eyes widened. Her red lips pouted. Moura was registering indignation, consciously doing so very prettily too; and the realisation of this was something that whipped Cat to even greater fury.

"I've as much right to be here," Moura said, "as you have."

Cat nodded towards Charlie. "Not with his arm around you, you haven't."

"Who says so?" Moura gave a pert toss of her head. Her eyes, provocatively smiling, slid a sideways look at Charlie; and hotly through Cat's mind ran the words:

I've seen all this before – the way Morven Reid did it, the way she copied Morven, even though she was just a kid at the time. But she's bloody well not going to do it to me with Charlie!

She spoke aloud, her voice rising into a shout. "I say so!"

The hall had gone very quiet. From the street outside came a sound that was like the urgent ringing of a fire-engine's bell. Charlie began to speak, but his words were lost in this ringing noise. Cat would not have heard them anyway because, just at that moment, Moura began to laugh, head tilted backwards, white throat vibrating with the sound.

There was a gold chain around that white throat, a chain designed to match the earrings Charlie had been fingering. Cat's hand flashed out to grasp the chain. She wrenched. The chain broke, and dangled for a split second from her hand before she threw it contemptuously away from herself.

"Now laugh!" The challenge was hardly out of her mouth before Moura screamed, and sprang forward, fingers clawing for Cat's face. Cat ducked under the reaching arms, and came up with one hand slapping hard against Moura's face. She was screaming too, by then, although she was unaware of that fact.

168

All that did impinge on her as Moura staggered from the slap was the sight of the pretty face contorted to a rage that equalled her own, the black hair coming close enough to grab. Her hands shot out and fastened in that shining, hated black. She pulled, with savage joy in the pain she was inflicting. But Moura was strong, Moura was twisting to kick hard at her shins, and she was being kicked off-balance, falling, dragging Moura down with her . . .

It took half a dozen of the men to separate them in the end, and drag them to their feet with Kevin Reid and Charlie's brothers hanging on to Moura, while Alec and Rhona's brother held on to Cat. Kevin Reid shouted, as the two groups stood glaring at one another:

"She started it! The McPhie girl, she started it!"

"And what did you expect me to do," Cat yelled in answer, "with that bitch of a sister of yours cuddling up to *my* man!" Her eyes flew to Charlie. "And you," she added contemptuously, "you cuddling up to her. You that's told everybody you've marked *me* down."

"And so I had!" Angrily, his face flushing scarlet, Charlie took up her challenge. "But what d'you expect me to do when you turn me down flat like you did this morning?"

"I didn't turn you down. I just tried to tell you – "

"You just gave me a lot of double-talk. You just tried to find a way of not saying straight out that you wouldn't marry me. And then your daddy took you away before I could make you tell me why you wouldn't."

Everybody was crowding nearer now, everybody intently listening for Cat's answer. And, she realised, there was no way now of getting out of what she had to say. Her anger changed, became a cold feeling that told her she had no choice now except to be merciless in finally giving Charlie the reason why she could not accept the terms of a traveller marriage with him. She would not, she simply could not live in a way that meant sharing a trailer with Maggie Drummond's beaten face for her daily company, with Daddler reeling in full of whisky, shouting, breath stinking . . .

Words sprang into her head, words that echoed strangely out of the past, out of the mind of a small girl lying at night in a tent, unaware that it was the gift speaking in her. She faced Charlie squarely and spoke the words aloud, giving them the full weight of that cold, decisive anger.

"All right, if you want it straight. Your daddy's a drunk, and I won't share my life with a drunk. I'll never travel with your family, Charlie."

She was away then, before anyone could stop her, wrenching herself free of the holding hands, ignoring the cries that Rhona sent after her, pushing her way roughly past all those between herself and the door of the hall, running down the steps outside, running, running away from the pain of knowing that she was finished now with Charlie, finished forever with him . . .

There were four miles between her and the camp, four winding miles of unlit country road. A stitch in her side forced her pace down to a walk. She trudged on, with time beginning to wipe out all other feeling except fear of the surrounding dark; and was grateful when the head-lights of a car coming up behind her lit the stretch of road ahead.

She veered to one side of the road, giving the car plenty of room to pass. But the car did not pass. It drew to a screeching halt beside her. The door on the front passenger side was thrust violently open. A man tumbled out, hands reaching for her. She screamed in teror, and attempted a run that lasted only a few steps before she was grabbed from behind. A man's voice sounded over the noise of her screams. She was whirled round to face the owner of the voice – and it was Drew McPhie, her tall cousin Drew!

She tried to speak, to express her weeping relief. But Drew wasn't listening, Drew was dragging her towards the car, opening a door, pushing her into the back passenger seat. And Alec was there in the back of the car, with his arms around Rhona, and Rhona was weeping, and Drew was in the front pasenger seat again, yelling to the driver:

"Get on, Charlie! Put your foot down hard, man, *hard!*"

Cat struggled up to a sitting position; and dazedly, as the car shot foward, she asked:

"What's wrong, Alec? What's happened?"

"The camp." Alec spoke tersely, his voice low. "It's on fire. Some yobbos from the town attacked it. Threw petrol bombs at the trailers."

"Oh, no!" With wild visions of Jamie, her father, her mother, surrounded by flames, Cat's voice rose sharply in denial. "It can't be, Alec. It can't be!"

"It is." Alec nodded towards Charlie, hunched over the steering wheel. "Charlie there, he was in a right state after you barged out. Rhona and me took him out to the pub next door to the hall – like, you know, we'd thought we'd talk to him quietly, calm him down. Drew came looking for us there. Told us Big Andy had phoned the hall to tell us about the fire, to tell us to get back quick to

171

the camp. Charlie had his Vitesse handy, so we just piled into it."

"The fire brigade! Alec, did anyone – "

"Big Andy," Alec interrupted Cat's question. "He phoned them before he phoned the hall. They'll be there before us."

The bell – the sound of that fire-engine bell ringing . . . Cat leaned forward, hands gripping Drew's shoulders. The Vitesse was fast. The Vitesse would have them there in two minutes now, almost on the heels of the fire brigade. Intently she peered ahead through the windscreen. That glare in the sky – oh God, if she could see that glare already, the flames must be fierce, fierce!

The flames were fiercer even than she had imagined. The figures of the men running back and forward among them were black against their glare. She ran towards them, and was brought up short by her father, blocking her way, seizing her, hustling her over towards a group of womenfolk clustered around a figure lying on the ground.

"Keep away, keep away!" he was yelling as he ran her towards the group. "Jamie's safe, your Mammy's safe, but for God's sake, Cat, keep away from this lot!"

The figure on the ground was that of a woman, her clothes half-burned away, face so blackened that she was barely recognisable as Alec's mother, Lorna. Cat became aware of her own mother beside her, staring, as she herself was staring down in shock at the burned figure.

"What happened?" She turned to Ilsa, to the face that was so like, yet now so unlike the burned one of the sister lying there. Ilsa had Jamie clasped tightly to her. She answered Cat as if she were speaking to a stranger, her voice sounding flat, mechanical.

172

"Lorna's trailer was the first to get hit. A petrol bomb. It went up like a torch. She'd just got up from the camp fire when it happened, to go and have a look at wee Isobel. We couldn't stop her running into the trailer. The men managed to drag her out, but they couldn't – they couldn't – "

The mechanical voice broke down, became a human one that sobbed and sobbed; and Cat found her own horrified mind supplying the words her mother had been unable to utter. Rhona's baby was dead – burned to death!

The world reeled – the world of leaping flames and red-lit sky, of newly-arrived figures running from vehicles of every shape and size, of other uniformed and helmeted figures struggling with hoses, of horses rearing in panic . . . And noise – the confusion was shot with noise; swishing of water, yelling of voices, explosions, the cylinders of butane gas in the trailers were exploding with the heat. There was someone vomiting, somone near at hand, and screams – the horses were screaming their panic at the fire – no, oh dear God, no! it wasn't the horses! Cat clapped her hands to her ears. It was Rhona who was screaming, Rhona with three men trying to hold her as she fought like a madwoman to reach the smouldering heap that held her dead baby, while Alec retched and retched there on the grass . . .

There was an ambulance on the scene now, and stretcher-bearers kneeling beside Lorna MacDonald. Other figures appeared beside the three who were barely managing to hold the frantic figure of Rhona, and Rhona went quiet, limp – "as if somebody had given her a jag," Cat thought dully. The men among the travellers began to drift towards the group of their womenfolk, leaving everything now to the firemen, the professionals at dealing with tragedy. Cat stumbled towards the figure of her father, and he spoke as he clasped her to him.

"I have to tell you, Cat. Shuffler's dead. I shot him. I had to, lassie. He was trapped under the trailer, chained there so that he couldn't try to follow you to the town, and the whole thing was in flames. I tried to get to him. I tried and tried. But it was no use, and he was howling, near demented with fear and pain. So I had to get your Uncle Andy's .22 and kill him."

A dog's life was short, and she had always known that Shuffler would die before she did. But she'd promised him, hadn't she? She'd promised Shuffler that she'd never leave him, that she'd be there beside him when his time came. And Shuffler had understood what she was telling him. Shuffler had trusted her, and she was sure he had understood. Yet still she hadn't been there, after all, hadn't been there, hadn't been there . . .

"One shot, Cat. That was all it took." Her father was holding her at arm's length now, trying to read the expression on her face. "And it gave him a cleaner death than he would have had."

Her father, too, was in need of comforting, Cat realised. The break in his voice was enough to tell her that. Quietly she said.

"It's all right, Daddy. You did your best."

Jim's hands dropped from her shoulders. With his eyes travelling over the devastation all around them, he told her:

"It was just youngsters, you know, just kids in their teens. We saw them as they ran off. And look, look at the sort of thing they used." Bending, he picked up a jagged fragment of bottle glass. "Petrol bombs – see? Milk bottles filled with petrol, a rag stuffed into the neck, and a match put to the rag – so easy for them to make, eh? But look, oh look again, Cat! Just see what they've done with those things!"

But why? Why? Through the turmoil of other feelings in her mind, Cat heard the question insistently ringing, and watched forlornly as her father left her to join the group of men and boys surrounding the huddled figures of Alec and his father, Hamish MacDonald. Charlie, she realised, was one of the group, and she moved to stand beside him. Hamish had Alec cradled in his arms, and was trying to revive him with a sip of whisky. Alec's eyes were closed, his face white. Hamish persevered, pressing the neck of the bottle against Alec's lips. The lips opened, Alec swallowed, choked a little, then sat up, spluttering. Cat put a hand on Charlie's arm, and when he turned to her, she said:

"My daddy told me it was just youngsters that did it, Charlie."

Charlie shrugged. "That figures. Copying what they see on TV, I suppose. Throw the petrol bombs – flash, boom! Just like the way they do it in the war films."

"But why us, Charlie? We never did them any harm."

"What did that matter to them? Kids learn from their parents too, don't they? They learn to be scared of us, just because we're different from them. And that's quite enough to make us a target."

Charlie wiped a hand wearily across a face that was black with smoke. The hand was shaking, Cat noticed; and timidly she asked:

"Do you – do you want to go on being a traveller, Charlie? I mean, in spite of all this, you wouldn't think of giving up, would you?"

Charlie looked down in surprise at her. "Who, me? I'm a traveller born, aren't I? Never wanted to be otherwise. And I'm not going to let a few daft kids change my mind on that."

"Me neither!" In a sudden overwhelming rush of feeling for Charlie, Cat slipped a hand down to clasp his; and breathlessly she added, "Let's stick together, Charlie. We can work something out – can't we?"

Charlie looked down at her. "Sure we can, Cat." His fingers tightened on her own. He smiled, teeth white against his blackened face; and once again, with conviction as well as reassurance in his voice this time, he told her, "Sure we can!"

14

It was a strange time for them all, the days and weeks that followed the fire.

They were destitute, of course, so thoroughly had the trailers burned; but the farmer who had engaged them to pick potatoes housed them in one of his barns, and every other traveller family in the area came hurrying with as much food and clothing and bedding as they could spare from their own store.

The police came to investigate the fire-brigade's report that the fire had been an act of arson; and there was nothing of Sergeant McKendrick's bullying manner about these men. They listened carefully to all that could be told about the fire, then went away leaving grave assurances that they would soon have the culprits by the heels; and watching them depart, it seemed that Big Andy spoke for all of them when he exclaimed:

"Well, I'll be double-damned if they polis aren't for once on *our* side!"

More outsiders followed the police – people who had read a newspaper account of the fire and were shocked to know it had been a deliberate attack on the camp. They came from charities of one kind or another, all offering to help. But Dr Ballantyne, the little man with the kind eyes, was the first of them, driving up to the barn with a load of clothes and other stuff gifted by his organisation that was "interested in travellers"; and his eyes, when he saw for himself what had happened, were no longer kind.

He would come again, he assured them, just to see how things were going with them. And if they needed any further help – cash, for instance, to help replace the cars and trailers that had been burned – he would see what could be done about that. Word of the fire spread quickly, however, as news always does in traveller circles, and soon there were other travellers arriving at the barn – from just outside the immediate area, to begin with; and then, as the days slid by and became numbered in weeks, it was from farther and farther afield that those other travellers came.

It was money they offered, too, when they found that other needs had been taken care of, the money that Dr Ballantyne had foreseen would have to be obtained from somewhere. And, it seemed to Cat, there was hardly a day passed without some traveller family or another arriving at the camp and the man of the family stepping forward to hand over his contribution.

A few pounds, that was all it usually amounted to, a few worn and greasy notes counted out from pitifully thin bundle of other notes. But occasionally also, there would be a much larger contribution from a traveller who had enjoyed some recent windfall, or else was prospering in some business or other – as was Daddler Drummond was with his scrapyard.

"But what's money there for, except to be spent?" It was Daddler himself, after he had made his own generous contribution, who summed all this up for them; but behind the smiling agreement that answered his question, Cat sensed the movement of some deeper and more serious feeling.

It was true, certainly, that travellers spent what they

had and seldom took thought for the morrow. But travellers couldn't live at all unless they had wits, and skill, and brains, and one helluva lot of endurance too; unless, in fact, they were born survivors. Yet even that still wasn't enough for survival. Not without love, not without their strong ties of family. And as they were now, certainly not without the strength of fellow-feeling that was coming from those who weren't even blood kin to them . . .

Those, she thought, were the good things that followed the fire. And then there were the bad things.

There was the baby Isobel's funeral, with travellers coming from far and near for that, too, even though it couldn't be a real funeral – not with only a few bits of burned bone to be put into a little box and lowered into the ground without even a minister standing by to say, *This was Isobel.* It was Big Andy who spoke, instead; and Big Andy could whisper words that were magic to horses, but he was no good at making speeches. He wasn't even a religious man, either; and so it was his mother's words he used, Old Nan's words, the kind of thing she used to say when a child died.

"God is strong," Big Andy said. "The bairn is dead, but always in our hearts there will be a place for her; and God is strong. There will be green grass yet, in the fields. The bare trees will yet be green again with new leaf. There will always be a road to travel. God is strong, and there will yet be another bairn for us to love."

Cat found herself leaning against Charlie's shoulder, weeping, as they were all weeping at Big Andy's words – men, women, and children, all alike in their swollen and tear-streaked faces. And if they were this way, she asked herself, was it any wonder that Alec now seemed no more than the ghost of the Alec they had once known? Or that Rhona seemed to have gone altogether out of her mind with grief?

Visiting Rhona in hospital – that was the worst of the bad things that followed from the fire. Rhona was in a separate ward from the one where Alec's mother, Lorna, lay with her burned face and arms swathed in bandages; and every visiting day, after they had sat for a while with Lorna, they went along to this other ward. But Rhona, it seemed, didn't want to see anybody now – not even her parents, not even Alec.

With all of them she was the same, never speaking, her eyes always staring, staring, into some endless distance; and among themselves, when each visiting hour was over, they talked and worried endlessly over this strange silence.

"I'll speak to the doctor about her." It was Rhona's father, George McPhie, who came eventually to this decision. "I'll make him say straight out what's wrong with her."

"The chief doctor," Rhona's mother, Lizzie, insisted. "Make it the chief one, George."

But the chief doctor, it seemed, was a busy man. Or maybe he was just too grand to notice the traveller man who waited patiently, day after day, outside his office and in panic, at last, Cat had to admit to herself that the Rhona who lay so white and still in her white hospital bed was the Rhona of her vision on the day she had taken Dr Ballantyne's card from her. So it was up to herself to do something about that, wasn't it? Because if she didn't Rhona might die, she might die . . .

The card was gone now, of course, burned along with their pearling money and everything else in the trailer.

but she had long since memorised everything printed on it, and she had no difficulty getting through to Dr Ballantyne's number.

"Leave it to me." His reply, when she had babbled out her story, was quiet yet authoritative. "Just give me the number you're calling from, stay beside the phone, and I'll call you back. OK?"

"OK." Cat put down the phone, and crouched down to wait in the phone booth. Shuffler – if only she could have had him here for comfort now! But he was dead. Her Shuffler, the awkward one, her powerful, faithful Shuffler was dead. Head down on her knees, she wept, and wept again for Shuffler who was dead and for Rhona who might be dying . . . The phone rang, a hard, shrill sound in the confined space of the call box.

"Cat? Sorry I've been so long. It's taken a while to get things sorted out. But listen now. Here's the situation." Dr Ballantyne's distant, disembodied voice slowed its pace, became more distinct.

"The doctor realises, of course, that Rhona is in shock over the loss of her baby. But he doesn't know travellers as I do, doesn't know just how deep their family emotions run; and so he thought that a period of rest and some sedatives would be enough to let Rhona begin to recover. But I told him – I warned him, in fact – that the chances were she would die of grief; and I got my medical colleague here to back me up on that. So the hospital doctor had a talk with one of *his* colleagues, a psychiatrist in another hospital, and Rhona's going to be transferred there for the kind of treatment that'll bring her out of her state of shock. It's called electro-convulsive therapy – ECT, for short – and I'll keep in touch with you over the results. Are you listening, Cat?"

Yes, she was listening, and Dr Ballantyne was wonderful and the people at the hospital were wonderful and she couldn't wait to tell Alec and Uncle George and Aunt Lizzie and everyone else that Rhona wasn't going to die, but – Like a hot, burning sore that the balm of Dr Ballantyne's words had failed to heal, Cat felt her anger at those who had caused the fire throbbing through her relief at the news about Rhona.

Rhona had suffered, was suffering still. And for the rest of her life, Rhona's heart would carry the wound made in it by the death of her baby. And meanwhile, it seemed, there was no justice in the world, because the police had caught the kids who had fired the camp; and just because they were kids they wouldn't even go before a proper court and get the kind of hard punishment they deserved. They would come up, the police had said, in front of something called a Children's Panel –

And just be told not to be bad boys again, with a pat on the head, very like, to help them remember.

Bitterly, behind her thanks to Dr Ballantyne, the words echoed in Cat's mind; and bitterly again, a few days later, she spoke them aloud.

They were all in the barn at the time – all of them, even Alec, feeling cheered up by news of the first slow signs of improvement in Rhona's condition. Dr Ballantyne was there too, fulfilling his promise of keeping in touch with them after Cat's phone call. But Dr Ballantyne dropped out of the conversation once it turned from Rhona to the culprits of the fire and what the police had said about them. Dr Ballantyne had looked embarrassed when George McPhie had described in savage detail what he would like to do to them; and when the argument that followed became the general one that produced Cat's

182

remark, he rose to take his leave.

"Wait, now! Hang on a minute." Jim McPhie looked up with the request; and awkwardly, Dr Ballantyne returned to the wooden crate that had been his seat. Jim leaned towards him.

"You've seen those kids, haven't you? You told me you had."

"Yes, once." Dr Ballantyne looked around with his explanation. "I've a friend in this area who's a social worker, and I visited her today before I went with you to the hospital. Those kids were in the waiting room of her office. They're part of her case load, it seems."

"Tell them, then." Jim gestured to the others. "Tell them what you told me – about what those kids are like."

"They're more or less the age of your own girl." Dr Ballantyne nodded towards Cat. "Five of them. They all look much the same as one another – thin, all of them, with that sharp-nosed look you get in people who've been under-nourished all their lives. Poor kids, in fact – but not in the way that you people understand "poor". They've grown up with the kind of poverty that means damp houses and peeling wallpaper and stinking drains and rats in the baby's bed – the kind of no-hope poverty you get in town slums."

Dr Ballantyne paused to sweep the listening faces with his glance. "They were all dressed alike," he went on, "cheapest of cheap chainstore clothes, but flashy with it – punk hair styles, dangly earrings – that sort of thing. Pathetic."

"*Pathetic!*" Incredulously Cat echoed the word. "You can say that after what they did to us?"

Moura Reid nodded agreement with the incredulity in

183

Cat's voice, and shot her a look of sympathy. Moura had come rushing with all the others to help on the night of the fire. She and Cat had wept together over Rhona's baby, all thought of their fight banished by the overwhelming grief they had shared then; and like the ally she had been ever since, Moura took up the cudgels in support of Cat.

"Aye, you tell us. What was pathetic about those cruel little bastards?"

"Their lives; the kind of lives I've described to you." Gravely, refusing to respond in kind to the violence of Moura's challenge, Dr Ballantyne answered. "They looked like creatures from some kind of hell − a hell of dirt, and ignorance, and violence. And yet they were human beings. Young ones; still young enough to be ashamed of what they'd done."

"How d'you know they were ashamed?" Suspiciously, his look hostile, George McPhie threw out the question. "Your friend, the social worker − did she tell you that?"

"They tried to deny it at first, she said. But they all had records, of course, and the police soon had them pinned with those bits of evidence of their movements that night, the petrol stains on their clothes, and so forth. So then they tried to brazen it out, swaggered about it, in fact. Then they were told about the baby. That broke them up. They cried, my friend said; sat in her office and kept telling her with the tears dripping off their faces, 'We didn't mean it, missis. We didn't mean it.'"

Jim McPhie spoke softly into the long silence that followed Dr Ballantyne's words.

"They killed a bairn − a wee baby that never did them an ounce o' harm. They sent the bairn's young mammy out o' her mind with grief, and left its daddy not much short of that state. They burned a woman so that her face will be scarred for life. They killed a dog that was heart of a young lassie's own heart. And for the rest of their days, to the very end of their miserable wee lives, they're going to have to bear the burden of knowing they've done all these terrible things."

Jim paused to look first at Cat, then at Alec's parents, and finally at Rhona's parents, before he finished:

"Can you think of any worse punishment for them?"

Nobody spoke. Cat felt her gaze falling away from the steady gaze of her father's eyes, and realised that the others were being similarly affected. The sound of the kettle boiling created a diversion that allowed Ilsa to change the subject by pressing Dr Ballantyne to stay for a cup of tea; and it was while they were all drinking the tea that Cat seized on the chance to slip out of the barn, so that she could have a final word in private with him.

Waiting there for him in the outside dark, she leaned against his car and rehearsed the speech of thanks she meant to give him for his help with Rhona. Her mind wandered from this to thinking of other things that had happened since the fire; and the sound of Dr Ballantyne's footsteps caught her in the midst of wondering whether her father's attitude to those five kids had been one of the good things or one of the bad ones.

Dr Ballantyne, she thought, would undoubtedly take the view that it was one of the good ones; but even so, once her stumbled thanks to him were over, she could not help posing the question. He had been on the point of leaving when she spoke, car headlights on, key in the ignition, and the light from the dashboard showed the surprise on his face.

"Of course it's one of the good things, Cat. One of the

best, the most decent-hearted things I've ever encountered. But I wasn't surprised by it, mind you; because there's no doubt about it, girl, that daddy of yours is a remarkable man."

"So are you!"

Cat hadn't meant to say this. The words just came blurting out on impulse, and Dr Ballantyne was embarrassed by them.

"Och, come on, Cat!" He looked away from her, fiddling with the ignition key. "I'm just a Civil Servant – a wee government official doing a wee job that calls for me to help the travellers in my area. That's all."

"It's not all. Because we're not in your area now, are we? I know that from the address on that card of yours. And you weren't in your own area the day I met you after the Game Fair." Dr Ballantyne made no answer to this; and after a moment, she persisted, "So why d'you do it, helping travellers like that, even when they're not in your area?"

Dr Ballantyne spoke at last, keeping his face averted at first, and then turning to look full at her.

"I can't say this without sounding as if I'm making a speech; but since you insist, here it is. You heard me once, years ago, telling your grandmother that I do what I do because I like travellers. And I'm telling you now that I like them because I can respect them. I respect them because they have a way of life that's built on resourcefulness, and sharing. I respect them for their determination not to be labelled in any way – in spite of the fact that the life they've created for themselves has caused them to be despised always, hounded often, and sometimes also to be the victims of violence and persecution. I respect them finally, because none of this would be possible for them if

186

they didn't have a deep belief in the individuality and importance of every man, woman, and child among them; and because, it seems to me, that belief is one thing of value that our modern world just can't afford to lose."

He stopped, still looking full at her; but Cat was now hearing other voices – those of her father and mother and Old Nan echoing across the years from a conversation at the side of Loch Ness.

The choice is yours, and whatever one you make, none of us will blame you for it . . . everyone has the right to make of their life what they want to make of it . . . every single life has its own importance . . . that's what travellers believe . . . still wondering what makes us different from other people, that's where the difference lies . . .

"Did you hear me, Cat?" Dr Ballantyne asked. "D'you understand now?"

"I do," Cat told him. "But there's one thing you didn't say. We learn early the kind of things you talked about."

"Teach them to your own kids, then!" Dr Ballantyne smiled at her, switched on the ignition, and drove away, leaving her looking after the car and thinking about the kids that she and Charlie might have. Because she *was* going to marry Charlie, and every penny she earned from now on would go towards helping him buy a trailer that would allow them to travel independently of Daddler and Maggie. That would be one way to work things out – the only way, in fact, because Charlie had already agreed to it. And he would certainly never agree to that other idea – the one she had cherished ever since Pibroch had died. Not Charlie with his love of cars as fast as the Vitesse!

But still, she could always go on dreaming about it, couldn't she? And even if Charlie teased her, she could maybe even talk sometimes about her dream. Slowly Cat turned back towards the barn, the picture of a trailer for Charlie and herself slipping from her mind and being replaced by the cherished dream-picture of a broad-backed grey pony plodding along between the shafts of a little cart.

The picture grew clearer, till she could see in it a man and woman walking one on either side of the pony; and at the tail of the cart a dog prancing alongside the figure of a child stepping jauntily along with face lifted to the sky and feeling free – free as a bird . . .

16

"I've got something for you," Charlie told Cat.

He was standing at the door of the trailer that he and Cat had bought to use after their wedding. The trailer was parked in the field that their farmer friend, Jack Brownlee, had said they could use for the wedding celebration; and on either side of them were the trailers of all the friends and family who had gathered for the event.

Charlie was hiding something inside his jacket, something that made a considerable bump. From her place in the doorway of the trailer, Cat glanced out over the field and thought how good of Brownlee it was to lend it to them just because they were faithful in working for him at the tailend of every tattie harvest. And how quickly everyone had gathered once she had sent out word that she wanted a Spring wedding because Spring would be the best time for herself and Charlie to start their travelling life together! She smiled down at Charlie, a teasing smile. Charlie was forever coming along and saying "I've got something for you," and it was always just something else to add to the stuff in the trailer.

"So?" she asked. "What is it you've got now?"

Charlie put a hand inside his jacket and drew out a puppy. It was black – *like Shuffler*" – Cat thought, her breath catching in her throat. Charlie handed the pup to her. It was a lurcher, cross-bred between a greyhound and a labrador, she guessed, just like it had been with

Shuffler. You could tell the labrador blood, at least, by that depth of chest and from the good, broad space between the ears; but the high set of its ribcage could only have come from a greyhound. But this pup was longer in the leg than Shuffler had been at the same age – about seven weeks, she guessed again; and when she put it on the ground there was none of the awkwardness of gait that had given Shuffler his name. She squatted down to watch the pup run, and Charlie asked:

"What'll you call him, Cat?"

"He'll be fast," she said. "With that length of leg, I'm pretty sure he'll be fast. I'll call him 'Strider'."

"Cat – " Charlie paused, and she looked up to see him flushing in embarrassment.

"It's all right, Charlie!" Swiftly she rose to face him. "I know you weren't thinking he could take Shuffler's place – and that you didn't mean it that way."

Charlie gave a nod of relief. "I hoped you'd see that. But it's still not right for you not to have a dog. And that's a good 'un. I had to search hard before I got such a good one for you."

She smiled at him. "Thanks, Charlie. I know that too. I've learned more about you this past six months, in fact, than I ever knew before."

Charlie gave her an answering smile that broadened into a grin as he told her, "Aye. But wait till the wedding, Cat, before you think you know it all!"

There had been a certain amount of discussion over the form the wedding should take. Some had argued for a ceremony in the Registrar's office, because that would at least give Cat and Charlie their marriage lines to show if they got into some kind of tangle with authority, the way

190

such things could so easily happen to travelling people.

There were others who dismissed this with contempt, saying it was just a case of being afraid of the day you never saw. And why shouldn't the two young people just declare themselves married in front of all their friends, the way that had been good enough for their mammies and daddies, and *their* mammies and daddies before them?

Nobody, not even the oldest person there, spoke up for the much more ancient custom where the young people held hands and jumped together through a fire built specially high for that purpose. That had always been a dangerous business, and it did not need Lorna Mac-Donald's scarred face to remind them of that kind of danger.

But it was Cat herself, of course who closed the argument by saying that it was her wedding and she would have it no other way except with Charlie and herself simply declaring themselves to be married. And so fire there was, after all, but only the usual fire at the centre of the camp, with all of them dancing and singing about it, and fiddles scraping and accordions squeezing, and bottles of beer being passed from hand to hand, and all the young ones and the dogs racing and going mad with the excitement of it all.

"Just like it was at our wedding, eh?" Ilsa McPhie asked, and smiled at her husband sitting with Jamie on his knee. Cat came to flop down beside them, breathless after a dance, and Ilsa's smile became a little laugh as she asked:

"Enjoyin' yourself, hen?"

"What do *you* think, Mammy?" Cat sighed contentedly, with one highlight of the wedding after another flashing through her mind.

Daddler had been behaving himself – for this once at

least. That was one thing she had noticed. And she had noticed Rhona too, of course, looking thinner than before but still with enough spirit returned to her to join occasionally in the dancing. And Alec – it had been impossible *not* to notice Alec, still so tenderly looking after Rhona. Love birds . . .

Then there had been her own daddy, sending them all into fits of laughter with his out of tune bagpipes. And Big Andy leading out one of his ponies and drunkenly insisting he had taught the beast to count up to ten and trying to show them how. And the farmer, Jack Brownlee, dancing first with Morven Reid, then with Moura, bending his white head towards each of them and obviously overcome with their charms – how they had all laughed at that! And how they had all cheered when Charlie had suddenly called a halt in the celebrations and stood with his hand in her own while he said:

"I declare that you, Catriona McPhie, are my wedded wife."

Cat leaned forward, hugging her knees, and heard again in her mind the words *she* had spoken then:

"And I declare that you, Charlie Drummond, are my wedded husband."

A hand landed on her shoulder, gently shook it. Charlie's voice whispered, "Cat. It's time."

Cat rose and looked around her. The evening had faded into night, but everybody was still busy drinking, talking, dancing, laughing. Nobody would notice herself and Charlie slipping away. And even when they were missed, nobody would think anything of that – because that, too, was traditional, the young married folk slipping away together. And so the others would just go on celebrating – maybe for another day yet, or even another two days!

Hand in hand she and Charlie stole away from the field, and headed for the hill behind Brownlee's farm. They passed through the narrow belt of scrub wood at the foot of the hill and climbed upwards, past the place where they used to sit with Alec and Rhona at the end of their day's work picking potatoes, and up until they reached a point where some huge grey rocks had fallen together to form a sort of cave.

Inside the cave was dark, but they had no need of light to know of the sleeping bag lying there, the pillows they had placed beside the sleeping bag. Face to face they stood at the mouth of the cave, the camp fire a pinpoint of light far below them, the night folded like a soft grey blanket around them.

Cat found that her knees were shaking. Charlie put his arms around her and she could feel that he, too, was shaking. She rested her head on his shoulder, and for a long moment they stood like this before he led her into the cave and began gently to undress her.

It was warm inside the sleeping bag. Charlie's hands continued gentle; yet even so, he could not avoid causing her the pain of his first penetration. But she was as hungry for him as he was for her, so that she did not mind the pain; and the love-making that followed was as fierce and ecstatic for one as it was for the other.

The cave faced east, and it was sunrise light striking into it that wakened Cat the next morning. She sat up, realising in a dazed way at first that she was alone, that there was no sign of Charlie. Her mind cleared with the further realisation that he must have gone down to the camp to hitch up the trailer so that they could follow up their plan of driving away early that morning, before anyone else was awake; and instantly then, she was on her feet and reaching for her clothes.

Hurriedly she dressed, bundled up the sleeping bag and pillows, and set off down the hill. They would have a good day to start out, she thought, a day with the air fresh and full of birdsong. Below her the camp was deserted, with everyone still seemingly asleep. Nothing moved there except Uncle Andy's ponies – two of them, the two brown ones. But where was the third one, the grey, the one she had named "Cruachan" because, he had told her, he had bought it from a farm in the shadow of the mountain they called Ben Cruachan?

Cruachan, the grey hill garron, was her favourite; and it was with a slight feeling of disappointment in being robbed of a last look at him that Cat reached the scrubwood at the foot of the hill. She pushed her way through the scrub, her bundle of sleeping bag and pillows now loosened and trailing, and came out on to the path that ran between the wood and the farm. Cruachan was standing on the path, harnessed between the shafts of a small wooden cart. There was a tarpaulin flung over the contents of the cart, and all around it were hung the willow baskets that she and her father had made in the winter just past.

Cat pulled up sharply in her tracks, staring in speechless astonishment at the sight. Cautiously then, she advanced to the cart, and once again stood staring. It *was* Cruachan. Those *were* the baskets she and her daddy had made. But who – How had they come to be there? What did it all mean? A voice sounded from behind her – Charlie's voice calling:

"You're ready now, Cat?"

She whirled to face him, the sleeping bag and pillows

sliding from her grip. Charlie was coming towards her, carrying the black pup, Strider, in his arms. He was smiling. There was a sprig of gorse stuck in his cap, a sprig that was unseasonably in bloom with small, bright-yellow flowers. She swallowed hard, nodded towards the pony and cart, and asked:

"This? What does this mean?"

"It means we're ready to go, doesn't it?"

"But – But, Charlie – " Cat shook her head in bewilderment. "I don't, I just don't understand."

"It's easy enough." Charlie nodded towards the pony standing broad-backed and patient between the shafts. "Cruachan, there. Your Uncle Andy knows how fond you are of the beast. It's his wedding present to you. Your daddy made the cart, with some help from the other men. And your mammy, and my mammy, and all the other womenfolk gave you the stuff that's in it and packed it there for you."

With a quick flip of his hand he threw back the covering tarpaulin. "See! Everything you'll need for the travelling life."

Even pearling gear! As Cat's shifting gaze settled finally in a wondering stare at the glass-bottomed jug, the forked stick, and the long rubber boots she would need for her pearling work, Charlie bent to place Strider on the ground. He straightened, his hands full of sleeping bag and pillows, and packed these into the cart along with the basins, the pots and pans, the tent, and the rest of the stuff there. Carefully he fastened the tarpaulin back in position.

"Now!" As a last gesture, he picked up Strider and set him on top of the tarpaulin. "Now we *are* ready to go, eh?"

"But Charlie, we can't!" Appalled, Cat stared at him.

195

"I mean, *you* can't. This isn't the way you want to travel."

"It's the way you want." Charlie returned her look, his face serious now. "I've heard you talk about it often enough, about that dream you have of travelling again the way you used to travel when you were a kid. And I'll tell you something, Cat. I know you well enough now to know that, with you, it's more than a dream. It's something so strong in you that you'll do it, some day. You'd even leave me to do it – "

"I wouldn't!" Wildly, Cat interrupted. "I wouldn't do that, Charlie."

Charlie sighed. "Aye, that's what you say now. But you can't give up the dream, can you, Cat?"

He was looking full at her, his face as honest and open as always; and, she found, she could not meet that honest look. Because it was true, the thing he had said. She could not give up the dream; and so, even although she had always refused to admit it to herself, she had to agree now that there was bound to come a day when she would leave him. But that day could be far off yet, couldn't it? And so why should Charlie suffer, meanwhile, because of it? He had come close to her, was reaching a hand to turn her averted face to his own, quietly telling her:

"And as for me, Cat, I'd a lot sooner set off with you now than be left to eat my heart out when the dream does get too strong for you."

With a quick movement away from her, he swung up on to the cart.

"No, Charlie!" Cat caught hold of the edge of the cart, and looked up at him with all the arguments she had once thought he would use against travelling her way springing clearly to her mind. "You deal in cars, Charlie, fast cars. How're you going to do that from a pony and trap?"

"There'll be towns on our way, and plenty of chances for me to put through a few quick deals."

"But beyond the towns – in the wild land where I'd like to go?"

"Fishing for pearls – what's wrong with that? I've always fancied the gamble in trying for a really good pearl."

"But when there's no shops, Charlie, and no money either – what then?"

Charlie began to grin. "You're not Poacher McPhie's lassie for nothing!"

"That's true. But it's old-fashioned to travel this way. You don't want people to laugh at you, do you, for being old-fashioned?"

"Nobody laughs at me and gets away with it. You know that, Cat. So why *should* I mind?"

"Well, maybe so. But that still doesn't tell me you're sure, really sure, that you want it to be like this."

"You wouldn't have seen me here at all this morning if I hadn't been dead sure of that!"

Charlie's voice was firm, his expression determined. But still – "You're forgetting the winter," she persisted. "The winter'll be cold, Charlie. It's always cold in a tent in winter."

"And you're forgetting something else, Cat." Charlie had begun to smile again. "We've got the trailer to come back to, and Brownlee's field to park it in. And by the time winter comes, my girl – if I did my work aright last night in the cave – I think that you and the bairn that's in you will be glad of the trailer."

Cat glanced from Charlie's smiling face to the camp still asleep in the brightness of the April morning. So it wasn't quite the one-sided bargain it had seemed, she thought. And she did so want to take advantage of it. She turned back to look at Charlie again. He bent towards her, smiling, one hand held invitingly out to her. The sprig of flowering gorse in his cap sent a whiff of scent across her nostrils; and suddenly she found she was laughing, with her hand accepting the grasp that swung her up to sit beside him, and through her laughter she was asking:

"What's the idea of wearing that in your cap?"

"You should know!" Charlie was laughing too, now. "I told you it once already, but you've proved it now. *When gorse is out, it's kissing time!*"

"Oh, Charlie!" Blushing, she turned to pick up the pup, Strider. Charlie reached for the reins, and asked:

"Which way, then?"

Cat looked along the path that bounded the scrub wood. *Trust the gift.* That was what her mammy had once said. And the gift had told her she would stand some day in Old Nan's enchanted land with Charlie's arm around her.

"North," she said. "We'll go north, Charlie."

Strider was shivering, needing something more than his own puppy warmth to protect him from the morning air. She held him close, pressing her face against his soft black coat, smiling at the lick of gratitude he gave her. Charlie urged the pony along the path beside the scrub; and at the end of the scrub he swung the cart left, on to the northbound road.

A Sound of Chariots

MOLLIE HUNTER

Bridie McShane grew up in a village in the Lowlands of Scotland after World War I, the noisiest, most spirited and also the most sensitive of five children. Her father, a veteran of the war, died when she was nine, and Bridie was shattered by grief. She was also possessed by the consciousness of time passing and the reality of her own eventual death, and haunted by the sound of 'Time's winged chariot hurrying near.' But Bridie was a gifted child, and gradually she was able to come to terms with her grief through her desire to be a writer.

'This moving story, told with deliberate simplicity, is shot through with tenderness and insight.'   *Glasgow Herald*

'An exceptional book which shines light on the clouds of glory without dispelling them.'   *Sunday Telegraph*

'Tough, yet tender, humorous, yet tragic, sometimes horrific yet always compassionate.'   *Times Literary Supplement*